A wedding dilemma:

What should a sexy, successful bachelor do
if he's too busy making millions to find a wife?
Or if he finds the perfect woman, and just *has* to
strike a bridal bargain....

The perfect proposal:

The solution? For better, for worse, these grooms
in a hurry have decided to sign, seal and deliver
the ultimate marriage contract...to *buy* a bride!

CONTRACT BRIDES

From paper marriage...to wedded bliss!

Look out for our next CONTRACT BRIDES story,
coming next month in Harlequin Romance®:
His Hired Bride by Susan Fox
On sale June 2005, #3848

Jessica Steele lives in a friendly Worcestershire village in England with her super husband, Peter. They are owned by a gorgeous Staffordshire bullterrier called Florence, who is boisterous and manic, but also adorable. It was Peter who first prompted Jessica to try writing and, after the first rejection, encouraged her to keep on trying. Luckily, with the exception of Uruguay, she has so far managed to research inside all the countries in which she has set her books, traveling to places as far apart as Siberia and Egypt. Her thanks go to Peter for his help and encouragement.

Jessica Steele's classic love stories will whisk you into a world of pure romantic excitement. Get ready to be swept off your feet by perfect English gentlemen!

Books by Jessica Steele

VACANCY: WIFE OF CONVENIENCE

Jessica Steele

HARLEQUIN®

TORONTO • NEW YORK • LONDON
AMSTERDAM • PARIS • SYDNEY • HAMBURG
STOCKHOLM • ATHENS • TOKYO • MILAN • MADRID
PRAGUE • WARSAW • BUDAPEST • AUCKLAND

ISBN 0-373-03839-9

VACANCY: WIFE OF CONVENIENCE

First North American Publication 2005.

Copyright © 2005 by Jessica Steele.

This edition published by arrangement with Harlequin Books S.A.

www.eHarlequin.com

Printed in U.S.A.

CHAPTER ONE

SHE had first seen him at her father's funeral, and had not expected to see him again. But here he was standing in front of her, tall, as she remembered, dark-haired and somewhere in his middle thirties.

Colly had not had the chance then to learn who he was; her stepmother of two years, only five years older than her, had monopolised him as they stood at the crematorium after the service. 'Do come back to the house for some refreshment', Colly had clearly heard Nanette urge.

He had suavely declined, looked as if he might come over to Colly to offer his condolences, but she had been button-holed by someone else and had turned away. He spoke to her now, though, apologising that Mr Blake—the man she was at the Livingstone building to see—was unfortunately incapacitated that day.

'Silas Livingstone,' he introduced himself. She had not known his name; he obviously knew hers. 'If you could hang on here for ten minutes, I'll be free to interview you in his stead.'

'Would you rather I made another appointment?' She would prefer not to do that. She was nervous enough about this interview as it was, and was unsure if she would ever have the nerve to come back.

'Not at all,' he replied pleasantly. 'I'll see you in a short while,' he added, and was already on his way to the adjoining office.

'Would you like me to wait elsewhere?' Colly asked the smart, somewhere in her late thirties PA, who appeared to be handling at least three tasks at one and the same time.

'Better not,' Ellen Rothwell replied with a kind smile. 'Mr Livingstone has a busy day. Now that he's found a slot for you, he'll want you to be where he expects you to be.'

Colly smiled in return but decided to say nothing more. She found it embarrassing enough as it was that apparently, so Ellen Rothwell had explained, Vernon Blake's present secretary had phoned around all the other applicants to cancel today's appointments. But, on phoning Colly's home at the start of business that day, had been informed that she was out and that there was no way of contacting her.

She had known that her stepmother had a spiteful streak. To deliberately refuse to call her to the phone when she had been in all the time only endorsed that fact.

Colly held back a sigh and tried to direct her thoughts to the forthcoming interview. Vernon Blake was the European Director at Livingstone Developments, and was looking for a replacement multilingual senior secretary. The salary advertised was phenomenal and, since Nanette wanted her to move out, would, if Colly were lucky enough to get the job, enable her to rent somewhere to live and be independent.

That had been her thinking at the time of spotting the advert. Never again would she be dependent on anyone. She had read the advert again. 'Multilingual senior secretary.' What was so difficult about that? She could, after all, type. And, though a little rusty with her languages, she had at one time excelled in French and Italian, and had scraped through with a pass mark in Spanish and German. So what else did a multilingual secretary need?

Watching Ellen Rothwell expertly deal with telephone calls, take notes in rapid shorthand and then calmly and charmingly sort out what seemed to be some sort of a problem, Colly realised that there was a lot else to being a secretary. And what experience of being a secretary did she have? Absolutely none!

She almost got up then, made her excuses, and bolted. Then

she remembered why she wanted this job that paid so much. Very soon she would be homeless. And she, who had never had paid work in her life, desperately needed some kind of well-paid employment.

It hurt that her father had left his will the way that he had. His twenty-eight-year-old widow had inherited everything; his daughter nothing. He had a perfect right to leave his money and property to whoever he cared to, of course. But she, his only child, his housekeeper since the last one had walked out seven years ago, was now about to lose the only home she had ever known. Not that it felt like home any more.

Colly had been little short of staggered when, just over two years ago now, her dour, often grumpy parent had gone all boyish over the new receptionist at his club.

The first Colly had got to suspect that he was seeing someone was when he'd suddenly started to take an interest in his appearance. She'd been glad for him. Her mother had died when Colly was eight—he had been unhappy for far too long.

Her pleasure for him had been tinged with dismay, though, when a short while later he had brought the blonde Nanette home—Nanette was about forty years his junior! 'I've been so longing to meet you!' the blonde twenty-six-year-old had trilled. 'Joey has told me such a lot about you.'

Joey! Her staid father, Joseph, was *Joey*! For his sake, Colly smiled and made her welcome and tried not to see the way Nanette's eyes swept round the room taking inventory of anything valuable.

Had Colly secretly hoped that her father would still be as happy when Nanette backed away from whatever sort of relationship they had, then she was again staggered when, far from the relationship ending, Nanette showed her the magnificent emerald ring Joseph Gillingham had bought her, and declared, 'We're getting married!'

For the moment speechless, Colly managed to find the words to congratulate them. But when, adjusting to the idea that Nanette was to be mistress of her home, Colly mentioned that she would find a place of her own, neither her father nor Nanette would hear of it.

'I'd be absolutely hopeless at housekeeping,' Nanette twittered. 'Oh, you must stay on to be housekeeper,' she cooed. 'Mustn't she, darling?'

'Of course you must,' Joseph Gillingham agreed, the most jovial Colly had ever seen him. 'Naturally I'll continue to pay you your allowance,' he added, with a sly look to his intended, making it obvious to Colly that her allowance—not huge by any means and which, with increasing prices, went to supplement the housekeeping—had been discussed by them.

The whole of it left her feeling most uncomfortable. So much so that she did go so far as to make enquiries about renting accommodation somewhere. She was left reeling at the rent demanded for even the most poky of places.

So she stayed home. And her father and Nanette married. And over the next few months her father's new 'kitten' showed—when her husband was not around—that she had some vicious claws when things were not going quite her way. But she otherwise remained sweet and adoring to her husband.

Living in the same house, Colly could not help but be aware that Nanette had a very sneaky way with her. And within a very short space of time Colly was beginning to suspect that her new stepmother was not being true to her Joey. That Nanette plainly preferred male company to female company was not a problem to Colly. What was a problem, however, was that too often she would answer the phone to have some male voice enquire, 'Nanette?' or even, 'Hello, darling.'

'It isn't Nanette,' she would answer.

Silence, then either, 'I'll call back,' or, 'Wrong number.'

Colly could not avoid knowing that Nanette was having an affair when some months later she answered the phone to hear an oversexed voice intimately begin, 'Who was the wicked creature who left me with just her earrings beneath my pillow to remind me of heaven?'

Colly slammed down the phone. This was just too much. Nanette, who was presently out shopping, had, so she had said, been out consoling a grief-stricken girlfriend until late last night.

When a half-hour later Nanette returned from her shopping trip Colly was in no mind to keep that phone call to herself. 'The earrings you wore last night are beneath his pillow!' she informed her shortly.

'Oh, good,' Nanette replied, not in the slightest taken aback to have been found out.

'Don't you care?' Colly felt angry enough to enquire.

Nanette placed her carriers down. 'What about?'

'My father...'

'What about him?'

Colly opened her mouth; Nanette beat her to it.

'You won't tell him,' she jibed confidently.

'Why won't I?'

'Is he unhappy?'

He wasn't. Never a very cheerful man, he seemed, since knowing and marrying this woman, to have had a personality transplant. 'He's in cloud-cukoo-land!' Colly replied.

Nanette picked up her clothes carriers. 'Tell him if you wish,' she challenged, entirely uncaring. 'I've already—tearfully—told him that I don't think you like me. Guess which one of us he's going to believe?'

Colly very much wanted to tell her father what was going on, but found that she could not. Not for herself and the probability that, as Nanette so confidently predicted, he would not believe her, but because he was, in essence, a much happier man.

So, awash with guilt for not telling him, but hoping that he would not blame her too much when, as he surely must, he discovered more of the true character of the woman he had married, Colly stayed quiet.

A year passed and her father still adored his wife. So clearly Nanette was playing a very clever game and he had no idea that his wife had a penchant for flitting from affair to affair.

That was until—about six months before his sudden totally unexpected and fatal heart attack—Colly first saw him looking at Nanette with a little less than an utter doting look in his eyes.

He appeared only marginally less happy than he had been, though, but did during his last months spend more time in his study than he had since his marriage.

Her father had been a design engineer of some note and, though in the main largely retired, she knew from the top executives and first-class engineers who occasionally called at the house to 'pick his brains' that he was highly thought of by others in his specialised field.

And then, completely without warning, he died. Colly, in tremendous shock, could not believe it. She questioned the doctor, and he gravely told her that her father had suffered massive heart failure and that nothing would have saved him.

She was still in shock the next day, when Nanette sought her out to show her the will she had found when sorting through Joseph Gillingham's papers. It was dated a month after his marriage, and Colly soon realised that Nanette had been more looking for his will than sorting through, especially when, triumphantly, Nanette declared, 'What a little pet! He's left me everything!' And, without any attempt to look sorry, 'Oh, poor you,' she added. 'He's left you nothing.'

That was another shock. Not that she had expected to be left anything in particular. Naturally Nanette, as his wife, if she were still his wife by then, would be his main heir. Colly realised she must have assumed her father would go on for ever; he was only sixty-eight, after all. And while he was not enormously wealthy, his income from some wise investing many years before was quite considerable.

It was two days after her father's death that Colly received a fresh shock when Nanette barged into her bedroom to coldly inform her, 'Naturally you'll be finding somewhere else to live.'

Somehow, and Colly hardly knew how she managed it, she hid the fresh assault of shock that hit her to proudly retort, 'Naturally—I wouldn't dream of staying on here.'

'Good!' Nanette sniffed. 'You can stay until after the funeral, then I want you out.' And, having delivered that ultimatum, she turned about and went from whence she came.

Feeling stunned, Colly couldn't think straight for quite some minutes. She had no idea what she would do, but heartily wished her uncle Henry were there to advise her.

Henry Warren was not a blood relative, but her father's friend, the 'uncle' being a courtesy title. She had known him all her life. He was the same age as her father but, newly retired from his law firm, he had only last week embarked on an extended holiday. He did not even know that his friend Joseph had died.

Not that the two had seen very much of each other since Joseph's remarriage. Her father's trips to his club had become less and less frequent. And Henry Warren seldom came to the house any more. It was because of their friendship that her father had always dealt with a different firm of solicitors, believing, as he did, that business and friendship did not mix. But Colly's first instinct was to want to turn to Uncle Henry.

But he was out of the country, and as her initial shock began to subside she realised that there was no one she could turn to for help and advice. She had to handle this on her own. She had no father, and no Uncle Henry—and Nanette wanted her out.

Hot on the heels of that realisation came the knowledge that she barely had any money—certainly not enough to pay rent for more than a week or two on any accommodation she might be lucky enough to find. That was if prices had stayed the same in the two years since she had last looked at the rented accommodation market.

She was still trying to get her head together on the day of her father's funeral.

She clearly recalled seeing Silas Livingstone there—his name now known to her. How Nanette managed to look the grieving widow while at the same time trying to get her hooks into Silas Livingstone was a total and embarrassing mystery to Colly. He and another tall but older man had gone to his car and had left straight after paying their respects at the crematorium anyhow, so Nanette's invitation to 'come back to the house' had not been taken up.

Having applied for a job with Livingstone Developments, Colly had done a little research into the company. And, on thinking about it, she saw that it was not surprising that the firm should be represented at her father's funeral that day. Livingstones were not the only big engineering concern to be represented.

She came out of her reverie to watch Ellen Rothwell handle whatever came her way. Secretarial work, it was fast being borne in on Colly, was more than just being able to type!

She had known that, of course. But supposed she must still be suffering shock mixed in with stress, strain and grief for her father, as well as a helping of panic thrown in, that, on seeing the advertisement for a multilingual senior secretary, and believing she could fulfil the multilingual part without too much trouble, she had applied.

She watched Ellen Rothwell for another thirty seconds, and realised more and more that she must have been crazy to apply. Colly got to her feet, ready to leave, but just then the door to Silas Livingstone's office opened and there he was, a couple of yards away—so close, in fact, that she could see that his eyes were an unusual shade of dark blue.

'Come through,' he invited, standing back to allow her to precede him into his large and thickly carpeted office. She was five feet nine—and had to look up to him. She had been about to leave, but found she was going into his office. He followed her into a large room that housed not only office furniture but had one part of the room—no doubt where he conducted more relaxed business—given over to a coffee-table and several padded easy chairs. He closed the door behind them and indicated she should take a seat to the side of his desk. 'I was sorry about your father,' he opened.

So he knew who she was? 'Thank you,' she murmured.

'Columbine, isn't it?' he asked, she guessed, since he had her application form in front of him, more to get her to feel at ease before they started the interview.

'I'm called Colly,' she replied, and felt a fool when she did, because it caused her to want to explain. 'I thought, since I was applying—formally applying—for the position with Mr Blake that I should use my full name—er—formal name.' She was starting to feel hot, but did not seem able to shut up. Nerves, she suspected. 'But Columbine Gillingham is a bit of a mouthful.' She clamped her lips tight shut.

Silas Livingstone stared at her and seemed glad that she had at last run out of breath. But, when she was getting ready to quite dislike him, he gave her a pleasant look and agreed, 'It is, isn't it?' going on, 'I stopped by Vernon Blake's office earlier. His present secretary said everything was running smoothly in his absence with the exception of an interviewee, Columbine Gillingham, who could not be contacted. Your father's obituary mentioned he had a daughter Columbine—I didn't think there would be two of you.'

It was her turn to stare at him. Was that why he had decided to interview her himself—because of her connection with her father? But there was no time to ask, and she supposed it was irrelevant anyway, because, obviously a man with little time to spare, Silas Livingstone was already in interview mode.

'What secretarial experience have you?' he enquired, glancing down at her application form as if trying to read where, in invisible ink, it was stated she had any office experience at all.

She felt hot again. 'I'm a bit short of actual secretarial experience,' she felt obliged to reply, wondering anew at her temerity in actually applying for the senior secretarial post. 'But my languages are good. And—and I type quite fast.'

He leaned back in his chair, his expression telling her nothing. 'How fast?' he enquired politely.

'How fast?' she echoed.

'Words per minute.' He elucidated that which any secretary worthy of the name would know. And, clearly already having formed a picture of her secretarial expertise—or lack of it, 'Any idea?' he asked.

She had no idea. Could not even give him a hint. She sat up straighter. 'Shall I leave?' she offered proudly.

He shook his head slightly, but she was unsure whether it was at her non-statement of work experience there before him or whether he was telling her that *he* would decide when the interview was over.

'Have you ever had a job?' He looked straight into her wide green eyes and asked directly.

'Er—no,' she had to admit. But quickly added, 'I kept house for my father. When I left school I took over the housekeeping duties until…'

'Until he remarried?' Again that direct look.

'I… My father's new wife preferred I should continue to look after everything.' Heavens, how lame that sounded!

'So you have never had an actual job outside of the home?'

Keeping house had kept her pretty busy. Though there was her interest in art. 'I usually help out at an art gallery on a Tuesday,' was the best she could come up with. She had visited that particular gallery often enough over the years to get to know the owner, Rupert Thomas, who at one time had asked her to 'hold the fort' for him when he'd had to dash out. From there it had grown and, today being Tuesday, she would normally be doing a bit of picture-dusting, a bit of invoicing, a bit of dealing with customers, not to mention making Rupert countless cups of coffee were he around.

'Is this paid employment?' Silas Livingstone wanted to know.

She was feeling uncomfortable again, and knew for sure that she should never have come. 'No,' she admitted.

'Have you ever worked in paid employment?'

'My father gave me an allowance,' she mumbled. She was unused to talking about money; it embarrassed her.

'But you've never earned—outside of the home?' he documented. Then abruptly asked, 'Tell me, Columbine, why did you apply for this job?'

He annoyed her. He clearly could not see why, with her lack of experience, she had bothered to put pen to paper. She couldn't see either—now. But his formal use of Columbine niggled her too. So much so that she was able to overcome her embarrassment about money to tell him shortly, 'I am not my father's heir.' She locked antlers with Silas Livingstone— and would not back down. But she did not miss the glint that came to his eyes.

'Your father left you something, though? Left you provided for?' he did not hesitate in asking.

Colly did not want to answer, but rather supposed she had invited the question. 'He did not,' she answered woodenly.

'I thought he had money?'

'You thought correctly.'

'But he left you—nothing?'

'Nothing.'

'The house?'

'I need to find somewhere else to live.'

There was a sharp, shrewd kind of look in those dark blue eyes as he looked at her. 'Presumably the new Mrs Gillingham did quite nicely,' he stated—and Colly knew then that, while her father had been blind to the taking ways of Nanette, Silas Livingstone, within the space of the few minutes he had been in conversation with her at the crematorium, had got her measure.

But Colly was embarrassed again, and prepared to get to her feet and get out of there. It went without saying that she had not got the job. He must think her an idiot to have ever applied for the post in the first place. All she could do now was to try to get out of there with some shred of dignity intact.

She raised her chin a proud fraction. 'Thank you for seeing me, Mr Livingstone. I applied for the job because I need to work, and not from some whim…'

'Your allowance is stopped?' He said it as if he knew it for a fact. 'You need to finance yourself?'

'I need a job that pays exceptionally well if I'm to live in a place of my own and be self-sufficient. But…'

'You're looking for somewhere to rent?'

'That's one of my first essentials,' she confirmed. 'That and to be independent. I intend to make a career for myself. To—'

She broke off when Silas Livingstone all at once seemed to be studying her anew. There was certainly a sudden kind of arrested look in his eyes, an alertness there, as if some thought had just come to him.

But even while she was scorning such a notion she could not deny he seemed interested in what she was saying. 'What about men-friends?' he asked slowly. 'You obviously have men-friends,' he went on, flicking a brief glance over her face and slender but curvy figure. 'Where do they come into your career-minded intention to be independent?'

She had thought the interview was over, and had no idea where it was going now. But since she had told this man so much, without ever having intended to—it spoke volumes for his interviewing technique—there seemed little point in holding back now. 'My father saw fit to leave everything to his new wife, and that was his prerogative. But it was a shock to me just the same, and it has made me determined to never be dependent on anyone ever again.' She went to get to her feet, but Silas Livingstone was there with another question.

'You have one man-friend in particular?' he enquired.

'Right now I have no interest in men or even dating,' she replied. 'I...'

'You're not engaged?'

'Marriage is the last thing on my mind.'

'You're not thinking of settling down, or living with some man?'

'Marriage, men or living with one of them just doesn't enter my plans,' she answered. 'I'm more career-minded than husband-minded. I want to be independent,' she reiterated. She had never been interviewed for a job before, so supposed being asked such detailed and personal questions must be all part and parcel of a job interview, but to her mind the interview was over. 'I apologise for taking up so much of your time,' she began, prior to departing. 'I thought when I applied for the job that I would be able to do it. It was never my intention to waste Mr Blake's time—or yours. But, since I obviously haven't got the job, I won't waste any more of it.'

She got up from her chair—but, oddly, Silas Livingstone motioned that she should sit down again. She was so surprised by that—she'd have thought he could not wait for her to be gone—that she did in fact sit down.

'I'm afraid you haven't the level of experience necessary to work for Vernon Blake,' Silas Livingstone stated. 'But,' he went on, before she could again start to wonder why, in that case, she had sat down again, 'there is the possibility of something else that might be of interest.'

Colly's deflated spirits took an upturn. While it was fairly certain that this other job would not pay as well as the one advertised, there was hope here that she might find a job that would lead to better things. Why, a company of Livingstone Developments' size must employ hundreds of office staff. Why hadn't she thought of that? She had a brain, there must be quite a few other jobs she could do!

'I'd be interested in anything,' she answered, trying not to sound too eager, but ruining it by adding, 'Absolutely anything.'

He silently studied her for what seemed an age. Studied her long and hard, before finally replying, 'Good.'

'What sort of work is it? I'm fairly good with computers. Or perhaps it's something to do with translating? I'd—'

'It's a—newly created post,' he cut in. 'The details haven't been fully thought through yet.' Again he seemed to study her, his eyes seeming to take in everything about her. 'Perhaps you'd be free to join me for lunch—say, Thursday?'

'Lunch?' she repeated. Was this the way of interviews?

He did not answer, but opened a drawer and withdrew what appeared to be a desk diary and began scanning it. But even while she was getting her head around the notion of lunching with this man while he told her more fully the details of this new vacancy he was shaking his head.

'By the look of it lunch is out for the next couple of weeks.' That was a relief. Personable though the man was, not to say downright good-looking, she somehow felt oddly reluctant to have lunch with him. Her relief, however, was short-lived, because, rehousing his diary, Silas Livingstone looked across at her. 'It will have to be dinner,' he announced. And, as cool as you please, 'Are you free this Friday?' he enquired.

Colly wasn't sure her jaw did not drop. She closed her mouth and stared at him. While admittedly she did not have all that much experience of men—this was a new approach. She might also not have any experience with general job interview procedure either, but she did not feel she had to be a genius to work out that this was far from the norm.

'Forgive me, Mr Livingstone,' she replied, striving hard for some of his cool tone. 'But I believe I've already told you that my interest rests solely with finding a job that pays well.' And, in case he had forgotten, she repeated, 'Men and dating just do not figure in my plans for the foreseeable future.'

'I heard you,' he replied evenly, adding—totally obscurely as far as she was concerned— 'That is an excellent start. But,' he went on, 'my sole intention in requiring you to have dinner with me is so we may discuss, in informal detail, this newly arisen—vacancy.'

Colly eyed him warily. Two years ago she hadn't had a suspicious bone in her body. But two years of living under the same roof as the devious Nanette had taught her not to take everything at face value.

'This *is* business?' Colly stayed to probe.

'Strictly business,' he answered, with not a smile about him.

Colly studied him. It made a change. But, looking at him, she somehow felt she could believe him. Could believe that this was not some newfangled way of him getting a date. And, looking at him, sophisticated and virile, she suddenly saw it was laughable that this man, who probably had women falling over him, would need to use any kind of a ruse to get a woman to go out with him anyway. Indeed, Colly started to feel a trifle pink about the ears that she had for one moment hinted that he might be interested in her in more than a 'business' way.

'Friday, you said?' she questioned finally, when he had given her all the time she needed to sift through everything.

'If you're free,' he agreed.

'This job—' she gathered her embarrassed wits together '—you can't tell me more about it now?'

'The—situation is recent, as I mentioned. I need to do some research into all it entails.'

'You'll have done your research by Friday?'

'Oh, yes,' he replied evenly.

She wanted to ask if the job was working for him. But, since he was the head of the whole shoot, she thought it must be. 'Bearing in mind my lack of experience, you think I would be able to do the job?'

'I believe so,' he replied, his dark blue eyes steady on her.

Colly got to her feet. She felt not a little confused, and hoped it did not show. 'Where shall I meet you?' she asked.

Silas Livingstone was on his feet too. Tall, unsmiling that she had just agreed to have dinner with him on Friday. 'I'll call for you at eight,' he stated.

She opened her mouth to tell him her address. Then closed it again. It was on her application form, and at a rough guess she felt that this man would not have missed that. In fact, she had a feeling that this man, who was obviously going to research into this newly created job pretty thoroughly before he offered it to her—or otherwise—never missed a thing.

CHAPTER TWO

HER first interview with Silas Livingstone had been on Tuesday. By Thursday of that same week Colly's head was beginning to spin from the effort of trying to pinpoint exactly what kind of job was in the offing that would be better discussed in 'informal detail' over dinner.

She still inwardly cringed whenever she thought of how, without a pennyworth of secretarial experience, she had applied for that senior secretarial job. It just went to show, she realised, how desperate she was for a job that paid well enough to afford her somewhere to live.

And that she would have to find that somewhere to live, and quickly, had been endorsed for her again last night, when Nanette had entertained a few of her rowdy friends. It was her right, of course, but the gales of laughter, male and female, that had come from the drawing room had impinged on Colly's sensitivities. Her father had barely been dead a month.

His widow had obviously decided to be the merry sort. If that was her way of grieving, so be it, but Colly had seen little sign of genuine grief. And all she wanted to do now, she mused, as she began to clear up the debris from the previous night's entertainment, was find a place of her own and get started on being solely independent. She knew then that whatever this job was, that was being newly created by Silas Livingstone, she would take it.

While it might not pay as well as that multilingual secretary's job, Silas Livingstone was well aware of her circumstances, so surely he would not be considering her for this new vacancy unless the salary that went with it was an adequate living wage.

By early Friday evening Colly had reasoned that, because her only skills were in keeping a well-run house, some small knowledge of art and an ability with languages, this newly created vacancy must involve the use of her languages in some way—which, plainly, was not secretarial. But, again, why dinner? It was almost as though the job was not in his office at all! As if it were nothing to do with office life—and that was why he was interviewing her in 'informal detail' outside of the office.

She was getting fanciful. Colly went upstairs to shower and get dressed, ready for Silas Livingstone to call.

Because this was to all intents and purposes a business dinner, Colly opted to wear a black straight ankle-length skirt of fine wool and a heavy silk white shirt-blouse. She joined the two with a wide suede belt that emphasised her tiny waist. She brushed her long brown hair with its hint of red back from her face in an elegant knot, and when she took a slightly apprehensive glance in the full-length mirror she was rather pleased with her general appearance. It was only then that she accepted that, with no other likely-looking job being advertised in the paper this week, she was pinning a lot of hope on this interview. She did so hope she would not come home disappointed. It was just that afternoon that Nanette had bluntly asked when she was leaving.

It was her luck that when, at ten minutes to eight, with a black wool cloak over her arm, she went downstairs to wait, she should meet Nanette in the hall. 'Where are you off to?' Nanette asked nastily, her eyes looking her over.

'I'm going out to dinner.'

'What about *my* dinner?' Nanette asked shrewishly.

Only just did Colly refrain from telling her that she had been her father's housekeeper, not hers. 'I thought you might be going out yourself,' she replied quietly; the atmosphere in the house was hostile enough without her adding to it.

'A—friend will be joining me later,' Nanette snapped. And,

an anticipatory gleam coming to her eyes, 'Don't disturb us when you come in.'

Colly went into the breakfast room to wait. It was a dark January night and she would see the car's headlights as they swept up the drive. Now, don't hope for too much. She attempted to calm herself down. There was every chance she might not yet be offered this job which could mean independence and a new way of life.

A minute or so later car headlights lit up the drive. Colly donned her cloak and, hoping it was Silas Livingstone and not Nanette's 'friend', left the breakfast room and went out to meet him.

It was her hopefully prospective employer. He left the driver's seat and came to open up the passenger door. 'Hello, Colly,' he greeted her amicably.

Well, that sounded friendly enough. She preferred Colly to Columbine. 'Hello,' she murmured. In no time she was seated beside him and they were motoring back down the drive. 'You found the house all right?' she asked politely. It was a nice house, in a very well-to-do neighbourhood.

'Not a problem,' he returned pleasantly, and matched her for polite conversation as he drove them to the eating establishment he had chosen, which happened to be a hotel.

He waited in the foyer while she checked her cloak. After taking a deep breath, her insides churning, she went out to join him. She gave him a smile. He smiled back, his eyes taking in her smart appearance. She had been out on dates before—but never with someone like him.

But this was not a date, she reminded herself as he escorted her to a lounge area. 'You're over your disappointment of last Tuesday, I hope?' he enquired as he waited for her to be seated.

'I blush whenever I think of my nerve in even applying,' she answered as he took a seat facing her.

He seemed to approve of her honesty. But, when she

thought that he would now begin to interview her for this other job, the newly arisen job, to her surprise did not, but merely commented, 'You're having a rather desperate time of it at the moment,' and asked, 'What would you like to drink?'

He went on to be a most courteous and pleasant companion.

'Mr Livingstone—' she began at one point.

Only to lose her thread completely when, 'Silas,' he invited—and kept up a polite flow of conversation as they transferred to the dining room.

He asked her opinion on sundry matters as they ate their way through the first course, and in fact was everything she could wish for in a platonic dinner partner. So much so that they were midway through their main course before she recalled that they were not here as friends but as prospective employer and employee.

'This job,' she inserted during a break in the conversation, realising only then how thoroughly at ease with him she felt. If that had been his aim he could not have done better.

'We'll get to that in time,' he commented. 'Is the steak to your liking?'

They were back in the lounge drinking coffee before Colly found another chance to introduce the subject of work without appearing to be blunt.

'I've very much enjoyed this evening,' she began politely, 'but...'

'But now, naturally, you'd like to know more about the vacancy.' He favoured her with a pleasant look, and explained, rather intriguingly, she felt, 'I wanted to get to know you a little before we embarked on a—full discussion.'

'And—er—you feel you have?'

'Sufficiently, I believe,' he replied, going on, 'I also wanted privacy to outline what I have in mind.' His mouth quirked upwards briefly. 'I hesitated to ask you back to my home.'

Her lovely green eyes widened somewhat. 'You're—um—

making this sound just a little bit personal,' she answered warily.

He considered her answer, but did not scoff that it was nothing of the sort, as she had expected him to. Doing nothing for her suddenly apprehensive feelings, he said, 'I suppose, in an impersonal way, it could be termed personal.'

'Do I get up and leave now?' she enquired coldly.

'I'd prefer you stayed until you'd heard me out,' he replied, his dark eyes fixed on her apprehensive green ones. 'You're quite safe here,' he added, glancing round what was now a deserted lounge. 'And we have all the privacy we need in which to talk this vacancy through.'

So that was why he had not gone into detail over dinner! A few fellow diners had been within eavesdropping distance should they have cared to listen in. 'So, you having assured me I'm not required to sing for my supper, I'm listening,' Colly invited, relaxing again, because should this conversation go in a way she did not care for she could decline to allow him to drive her to her home, and could ask someone at Reception to get her a taxi.

To hear that she was ready for him to outline the job was all Silas Livingstone was waiting for. Though, instead of outlining the work, he first of all stated, 'I've learned a little of you this evening, Colly. Sufficient, at any rate, to know that I should like to offer you this—position.'

Her heart lightened. Oh, thank heaven. She was on her way! Silas Livingstone must believe she could do the job, or he would not be willing to offer it to her. 'Oh, that's wonderful!' She beamed, her overwhelming relief plain to see. She might soon be self-sufficient, have money of her own and be able to afford somewhere to rent, and not beholden to Nanette for a temporary roof over her head.

He looked at her shining green eyes. 'You don't know what the job is yet,' he cautioned.

'I don't care what it is,' she answered delightedly. 'As long as it's honest and pays well. You wouldn't offer if—'

'Are things really so bad for you?' he butted in softly.

Colly took a breath to deny that things were in any way bad for her. Though when she thought of the dire state of her present finances, and then of Nanette's daily barbs that she pack her bags and leave, Colly couldn't think that they could be much worse.

'What sort of work would I have to do?' she enquired, ready to turn her hand to anything.

Silas studied her for a moment, not commenting that she had not given him a detailed account of just how awful things were at the only home she had ever known. Instead, he asked, 'Tell me, Colly, if it were not so very essential for you to find somewhere to live and to find a job with a salary sufficient with which to pay rent, what would be an ideal scenario for you?'

Again Colly found herself wishing she knew more about the usual interviewing techniques. Though, looking into the steady dark blue eyes of Silas Livingstone, she had an idea that he would not always follow the path of what was usual anyhow.

She looked away from him. 'I want to be independent,' she replied. 'I thought, a couple of years ago, that I'd like to have a place of my own...'

'But your father wanted you to stay on as housekeeper?'

'Nanette, the woman he married, she preferred that I stayed on.'

'And now, now that she has inherited the house and everything else, she wants you gone.'

It was not a question but a statement. And one that Colly could not argue against. 'So that makes my first priority to find somewhere to live and, of course, a job too.' She shrugged, feeling more than a touch embarrassed, but, it not needing any thinking about, she went on to honestly answer his question about her ideal scenario. 'From choice, I would prefer to do some sort of training. Perhaps take a year's foundation course while I looked into possible careers—or even go on to university.' She felt awkward again as she looked Silas in the eyes and confessed, 'I probably shouldn't be telling you this, but apart from an interest in art—though no particular talent—I have no idea what, if anything, I'm especially good at.'

Silas smiled then. He did not do it too often, but when he did she momentarily forgot what they were talking about. 'You have a nice way with you,' he answered. 'You have integrity, and I have formed an opinion that I can trust you.'

Colly felt a touch pink. Was that what all that non-business chat over dinner had been about—Silas gauging from her answers, her questions, her general demeanour, what sort of a person she was? My, but he was clever. So clever she had not had a clue what he was about. 'Yes, well,' she mumbled, just a trifle embarrassed. 'You must—er—trust me to have offered me the job.' She got herself more of one piece. And, on thinking about it, considered it was more than high time that she found out more about this vacancy. 'May I know exactly what the job entails? What my duties will be?' she asked.

Then she discovered she would find out what she wanted to know, but only when he was good and ready—because he had not finished asking questions of his own yet. 'First of all,' he began, 'tell me what you know about the firm of Livingstone Developments?'

Realising that since he was paying the piper she would have to dance to his tune, she replied, 'That's fairly easy. When I knew I had an interview last Tuesday, I made it my business to find out all I could about the company. I'd never been for an interview before,' she explained, 'so I had no idea of what sort of questions I should know the answers to.'

He accepted that as fair comment. 'What did you discover?' he wanted to know.

'I discovered that Livingstone Developments—only it wasn't called that then—was founded years and years ago by one Silas Livingstone.'

'Sixty years ago, by my grandfather,' Silas filled in.

'It was only a small company then—dealing with industrial equipment, I think.' She waited for him to interrupt. He didn't, so she went on. 'The firm expanded when your grandfather's son took over.'

'The firm made quite a progressive leap forward when my father took over,' Silas stated. 'Under his leadership the firm went on to become a leading international firm of consulting engineers.'

'And when, five years ago, Borden Livingstone stepped down and you were voted to be chairman, you led the firm onwards to take in the design and manufacture of more advanced engineering products.'

'You *have* done your homework,' Silas commented when she had nothing more to add. Then, giving her a straight look, 'All of which perhaps makes you see what a tremendous amount of hard work has gone on over the past sixty years to make Livingstone Developments into the much-respected and thriving company it is today.' His eyes were still steady on her when quietly he added, 'And what a colossal waste of all those years of hard labour, of effort, it would be if I can't come up with some way to prevent the company from sinking into decline.'

Startled, Colly stared at him. 'Livingstone Developments is in trouble?' she gasped, forgetting about her own problems—the company employed thousands of people!

But he was shaking his head. 'No,' he denied. 'We're thriving.'

The firm was thriving, yet sixty years of effort might be

wasted? It didn't make sense. There had to be an 'if', and a very big 'if' at that. 'But...?' she questioned.

Silas gave her an approving look that she was keeping up with him. 'A massive but,' he agreed, and went on, 'I had a meeting with my father on Monday. My father, I should explain, is the most level-headed man I know. I have never seen him panicky and have seldom seen him anything but calm. But there was no denying that on Monday he was extremely agitated about something.'

'Oh, I'm sorry to hear that,' she murmured politely. She discovered she would like to know more, but knew Silas would not tell her, and felt it went beyond the bounds of good manners to ask.

'No more sorry than I was to hear just why he was so disturbed,' Silas commented.

Her curiosity was piqued, not to say her intelligence—she was suddenly realising that Silas would not have brought her here and begun to tell her what he was telling her were there not some purpose behind it.

'I don't want to pry,' she began, 'but—'

And was saved from having to pry any further when Silas interrupted to inform her, 'All this has been a bit of a jolt for me, but I've had time since Monday to adjust. By the time I saw you on Tuesday I was beginning to acknowledge what had to be done, and that if the company was not ultimately going to go to the wall that it was down to me to do it.'

'I'm trying to keep up,' she commented. Fog? The fog was getting thicker by the minute.

'I'm telling you this in the strictest confidence, of course.'

'Of course,' she answered—whatever 'this' was.

'I'm also telling it very badly. Perhaps I'd better go back to the beginning,' he decided.

'It might be a good idea,' she conceded. If this was the way all job interviews went, she had to confess herself intrigued!

'To start with, my grandfather had a simply wonderful marriage.'

'Ye-es,' Colly said slowly, with no idea what direction they were heading in now.

'Sadly, my grandmother died six months ago.'

'Oh, I'm sorry,' she murmured sensitively.

'As you can imagine, my grandfather was devastated. But he at last seems to be coming to terms with his grief. Naturally we've all rallied round to try and help him at this dreadful time. My parents and my aunt Daphne—my grandfather's daughter—particularly. In actual fact, my parents spent the weekend with him at his home in Dorset only last weekend.' He paused, then added, 'Which is why my father rang me the moment he got home on Sunday. I wasn't in. He left a message saying it was of some importance that we meet without delay. I should explain—' Silas broke off what he was saying to note '—that my father does not use such language unless something of very great import is going down.'

Colly's brain was racing. 'It was to do with Livingstone Developments having some kind of sword dangling over its head?' was the best she could come up with.

'Got it in one,' Silas approved. 'My father isn't one to panic, as I mentioned, but he knew something serious was afoot when my grandfather told him that he wanted to talk privately to him in his study. My father came out from the study shaken to the core, still taking in what my grandfather had told him.'

Colly was desperately trying to think what any of this could have to do with her and this vacancy that had been created.

'Your grandfather needs a housekeeper?' She took a disappointed guess. It would be a job, and with accommodation thrown in. But did she really want to be a housekeeper for some elderly gentleman?

'He already has a housekeeper,' Silas informed her.

She was lost again. 'Sorry. I'll keep quiet until you've finished. Er—you haven't finished yet?'

'I'm getting there. The thing is that since my parents and aunt can't be with Grandfather all the time he spends many hours alone reliving the past. And at this present time, and with the loss of my grandmother so recent, he spends a lot of time thinking of her and their long years of very happy marriage. Which,' Silas said, 'brings us up to Sunday, when, in his study, my grandfather spoke to my father in terms of altering his will. Instead of my cousin Kit and I inheriting his considerable holding of shares in the firm between us—as I've always been lead to believe will happen—he intends to leave the whole basket-load of shares to Kit—if I don't buck my ideas up and marry.'

Colly blinked—and didn't know which question to ask first. 'You're not married?' was the first one to pop out.

'Never have been.'

'But your cousin—Kit—is married?'

'Has been this last ten years.'

'You're not engaged or living with anyone?' she questioned, more or less in the same way he had asked her on Tuesday.

He shook his head. 'No, nor likely to be.'

'Nor do you want to marry?'

'Definitely not. And, much though I'm fond of the old chap, I resent him, just because he has this sublime respect for the institution of marriage, attempting to force me to take a wife.'

'But unless you do you stand to be disinherited,' she reasoned. 'Join the club.'

'It's not going to happen.'

'Your father thinks he'll change his mind?'

'Very doubtful. My father's anxiety stems from the certainty that it *will* happen, and that all that he and I have worked for over the years will be as nothing if Kit gets a controlling interest in the firm. Which, with those shares, he most definitely will.'

'He's—er—not up to the job?'

'Don't get me wrong. Kit and I had a lot to do with each other during our growing years. I'm fond of him, despite his faults. But, as well as being no powerhouse when it comes to work—and that's being kind—he is far too easily swayed by others. Although he's already parted with some of the shares his mother gave him, he, like me, already has enough shares to guarantee him a seat on the board. But while we have a duty to our shareholders we also have a duty to our workforce. And I'm afraid Kit feels a duty for neither. It's a foregone conclusion that the ship will sink if he has any hand in guiding it.'

Colly did not know much about big business, but if Silas Livingstone thought it was so, she was quite willing to believe him. 'So…' she brought out the best her brain could come up with '…either you marry and inherit a sufficient number of shares to deny your cousin control, or you ultimately have to stand by and watch him ruin all that three generations of Livingstones have worked for?'

'Exactly,' Silas agreed. 'And while God forbid that anything untoward happens to my grandfather for years and years yet, I have to face the reality that he's currently aged eighty-four. Which is why I have determined that when that awful day comes, and he's no longer with us, I am not left hearing that unless I have been married for a year and a day the shares that should be mine have been inherited by my cousin Kit.'

By then Colly had forgotten entirely that she had only dined with Silas Livingstone to hear about a job he was now offering her. She recalled how wounded she herself had felt at the way her father had left his will. By the look of it, the shares Silas Livingstone had always been led to believe were half his would be willed elsewhere.

On thinking over all he had just said, though, she could

only see one way out for him—if he was dead set on keeping the company safe. 'I'm sorry, Silas,' she said quietly, 'but it seems to me that unless you're prepared to let the company fail you're going to have to get over your aversion to marriage and take yourself a wife.'

For ageless moments after she had spoken Silas said not a word. Then, drawing a long breath, 'That is the only conclusion I was able to reach too,' he said. And then, looking at no one but her, 'Which,' he added, 'is where you come in.'

She stared at him. 'Me?' she questioned, startled.

'You,' he agreed.

Her brain wasn't taking this in. 'No,' she said on a strangled kind of note as what he might possibly be meaning started to filter through. Then, as common sense swiftly followed, 'I'm sorry,' she apologised. 'For one totally absurd moment I had this weird notion that you were asking me to marry you.'

She laughed awkwardly, feeling that she had made a fool of herself. She was on the brink of repeating her apology, only, daring to take a glance at him, certain that he must be laughing his head off, she could see not one glimmer of being highly amused about him!

Colly swallowed hard. 'You weren't doing that, were you?' she asked, her voice gone all husky in shock.

'I cannot fault the idea,' he answered, his look steady, his expression unsmiling.

Did that mean that he *was* suggesting that he marry her? No, don't be ridiculous. Good heavens, she... Colly got herself more together. Whether he was suggesting what it very much sounded as if he was suggesting or not, she thought it was time she let him know her feelings.

'I don't want a husband!' she told him bluntly.

'Good!' was his answer, doing nothing for her feeling that she had just made one enormous fool of herself. 'I don't want a wife.' She wondered if she should get up and leave right now. 'But…' he added—and she stayed to hear the rest of it, '…you and I both have a problem, wouldn't you agree?'

'I know what your problem is,' she agreed.

'And your problem is that you need somewhere to live and the wherewithal to finance your training.'

'I hope you're not thinking in terms of giving me money!' she erupted proudly—and, oddly, saw a hint of a smile cross his features. 'I shall work for any money I—'

'Look on this as work,' he cut in quickly.

'This is the job you're offering me?' This wasn't happening; she'd got something wrong somewhere.

He took a long breath, as if finding her uphill work. She did not care. The whole notion was absurd—that was if she had got all this right. 'Try and see this logically,' Silas said after some moments.

Colly looked at him levelly, took a deep breath of her own, and supposed her reaction *had* been more instinctive than logical. 'So?' she invited, as calmly as she could.

'So in my line of business I have to work not for today but for tomorrow. Use forward planning techniques to the full.'

'As in marrying someone before your grandfather's will gets read?'

'Which hopefully won't be for years yet. But, yes. Had anyone but my level-headed father told me what the stubborn old devil intends to do I'd have paid scant attention.'

'But your father isn't one to panic unnecessarily?'

Silas nodded. 'I'd twenty-four hours to take on board what he said when the daughter of a much-respected man in the engineering world was there in my office—telling me she had been disinherited…'

'And that rang a bell?'

'Too true it rang a bell. You then went on to say how you needed a job that paid well, and how you were going to have to find some place to live, and I find I'm suddenly going into forward planning mode.'

'You—um...' She couldn't say it. She did not want to make a fool of herself again. Though she could not help but recall how he had asked her about men-friends, and if she were engaged or anything of that sort.

'I had an idea,' he took up. 'An idea that I've had since Tuesday to look at from every angle.'

'That idea being...?' she questioned, and waited, barely breathing, to hear whether she had been foolhardy to think he might be meaning what she thought he was so amazingly suggesting, or whether her brain, her instincts, had got it right.

'That idea being,' he said, looking at no one but her, his gaze steady, unwavering, 'to marry you.'

A small sound escaped her. Even though she had thought that might be what he meant, she could not help that small gasp of shock. 'Thank you for dinner,' she said, and stood up.

He was, she discovered, not a man to give up easily. He had cynically, no emotion in it, decided he would marry, case closed.

But he was on his feet too. 'Hear me out, Colly?' he asked of her. 'Neither of us wants to marry, so that's all in our favour.'

'How on earth do you make that out?'

'Neither of us is emotionally involved. And it's not as if we have to live with each other.'

'We don't?' she found herself questioning, even when she was just not interested.

He put a hand under her elbow and guided her from the lounge, waited while she retrieved her cloak, then escorted her out to his car. But instead of driving off once they were in his car, he turned to her and stated, 'You too have a problem, Colly.'

She half turned to look at him. 'I'm fully aware of that,' she answered shortly.

'And I'm in a position to solve your problems,' he said.

And before she could give him a curt, No, thank you, he was informing her, 'My grandfather owns a small apartment here in London where he and my grandmother stayed whenever they came up to town. He hasn't used it since her death, and he's said he will never again use it. But, because of his very happy memories of times spent there, neither will he part with it. He's asked me to keep an eye on the place, and I've stayed the occasional night there. But you'd be doing me a favour if you'd take it on. The place needs living in.'

Good heavens! 'You're offering me the tenancy?' she exclaimed, guessing in advance that she would never be able to afford the rent.

'What I'm offering, in return for you giving me a half-hour of your time and standing up in front of some registrar and making the appropriate responses when asked, is somewhere to live. I think you'll be comfortable there. Further to that, I'll undertake to fund any training you desire, be it a foundation course followed by university, or whatever you may wish to do.'

This was jaw-dropping stuff! She had come out with him for a job interview and had never expected anything like this! She just had to recap. 'In return for an "I will" you're prepared to…'

'On the day you marry me,' he replied unhesitatingly, 'I shall arrange for ten thousand pounds to be paid into your bank, with subsequent top-ups as and when required.'

'No!' she said, point-blank, and, nothing to argue about, she turned to face the front.

'Think about it,' he returned.

'I'd like to go home,' she told him woodenly. She was aware of his hard scrutiny, but was relieved when after some seconds he too faced the front and started up his car.

Neither of them spoke on the way back to her home. What he was thinking about she had no idea, but her head was positively buzzing. 'Think about it,' he had said—how could she not?

When she was desperate for somewhere to live he was offering her free accommodation! When she had a need to train for a career—and by twenty-three most women had a toe-hold on several rungs of the career ladder—he was offering to finance her career training!

She should be snatching his hand off. But—marry him! Colly knew that to marry him was something that she could just not do.

Having been silent all the way home, it was as if Silas Livingstone had thought to give her all the space she needed to get used to the idea. Because no sooner had he driven up to her front door than he turned to her.

'What's it to be?' he enquired mildly.

'I thought I'd given you my answer.'

'That was instinctive, spur-of-the-moment, an unanalysed reaction.' He shrugged that away. 'Marry me,' he urged.

'I—don't even know you!' she protested.

'You don't need to know me,' he countered. 'Just a half-hour—we need never see each other again.'

'No,' she repeated. 'I can't. I'm sorry. I know how very important this is to you, but—'

'You're right there,' he cut in abruptly, causing her to stare at him. But, relenting suddenly, 'I've had since Tuesday to adjust to the notion. Four days in which to weigh everything up, to mull it over and over, to get used to the idea before reaching the decision I have. On reflection, perhaps I'm not being fair, dropping it on you like this and expecting you to come back with the answer I want.'

She was about to reiterate that her answer was no. And that had she had those same four days it would not have made any difference—her answer would still be no—that she just did not need to think about it, or need to get used to the idea either. But Silas was no longer beside her. He was out of the car and had come round to the passenger door.

She stepped out and he stood with her for a moment on the gravel by the front door. He glanced down to where, in the light of the security lamps, her dark hair glowed with red lights. 'Think about it,' he said. 'Think about it and I'll call you. I'll phone you Tuesday evening.'

Colly looked up. His expression was telling her nothing. She opened her mouth to again tell him no, that she had no need to think about it, then realised that he was not in any kind of mood to take 'no' from her.

'Goodnight,' she said, and went indoors.

Saturday and Sunday passed with Colly still trying to believe that the conversation that had taken place on Friday night had actually taken place and was not some figment of her imagination. Had Silas Livingstone really suggested they marry? Had he really told her to think about it and that he would call her for her answer?

Whatever—his astonishing proposal did achieve one thing: her head was so full of it there was small room for her to take much heed of Nanette's spiteful barbs whenever they were within speaking distance of each other.

Though on Monday morning Nanette was at her most vicious. 'You still here?' she snapped when she eventually came down the stairs.

'I'm making plans,' Colly returned, without a plan in her head.

'You'd better make them pretty quick, then,' Nanette retorted, going on to inform her nastily, 'If you're not out of this house by the end of the week I'm having all the locks changed!'

'You can't do that!' Colly gasped.

'Who's going to stop me? Joseph Gillingham left this house to me.' And, with a triumphant smirk, 'It's mine!'

Not for the first time Colly wished that her father's lawyer friend Henry Warren were there to advise her. Surely she could not be barred from her home of twenty-three years? Be put out in the street—just like that! But Uncle Henry was still holidaying abroad, and to seek help from some other legal representative would take money. And money was in rather short supply just then.

How short was again brought home to her when, a little while later, she went looking for a flat to rent. Prices were sky-high! She couldn't so much as pay the first month's rent in advance for even the lowliest bedsit!

Silas Livingstone's proposal that she stand with him in front of some registrar suddenly started to have a weakening effect on her. She stiffened her backbone. She couldn't do it. Marry him? Take money from him? No, it was out of the question.

She returned to her car, but had no wish to return home. It was not home any more. She began to feel all stewed up— what other options were open to her? There were none. She replayed again that morning's spat with Nanette and could not get it out of her head. That was when Colly realised that if she dwelt on it many more times she might yet weaken completely. And she could not weaken. She could not marry Silas Livingstone.

On impulse she took out her phone. She would tell him now. She would not wait until tomorrow for him to call her. She would tell him now—while she still had the strength of mind.

She supposed she should have realised it would not be as simple as that to get in touch with him. He was a busy man. He had not even had any free time in which to take her to lunch last week, had he?

Though she did get through to his PA, and it was almost as if Ellen Rothwell had been instructed to put her through to him were she to ring, because the PA was most affable and informative when she apologised and said, 'I'm sorry, Silas isn't in right now. All being well, he should be in the office at some time between three and four if that's any help?'

'Thank you very much. I—er—may call back,' Colly replied, and, unable to sit still, she left her car wishing that it was all over and done with.

As she walked aimlessly about so she started to blame him. It was all his fault that she was in this stew. If he had taken her at her word on Friday she would not now be wandering around fretting the pros and cons of his whole astonishing suggestion anyway.

Not that she had thought too deeply about his side of things. Though it was plain that Silas must be more than a little desperate to have put the preposterous proposal to her in the first place. He, with his forward planning, could see everything he and his father before him—and his grandfather too, come to that—had worked for going down the drain if his cousin got his hands on those controlling shares.

He knew his cousin better than she, who had never met him. But surely this Kit person was not so bad as all that? If he were, then would Grandfather Livingstone really change his will in the married Kit's favour? She could not see it.

But suddenly then Colly was shocked into reconsidering. It had never dawned on her that she would be made homeless when her father died—but he had changed *his* will, hadn't he? And, when she might have been forgiven for not expecting to be left destitute, he had left her not a penny.

Feeling a little stunned, Colly began to wish she had not started to think about this marriage proposal from Silas's angle. Because now that she had she began to think of all those employees who would lose their livelihood, the shareholders who might have invested perhaps more than they could afford in the prosperous company—all of whom stood to suffer financially should Silas's worst fears come to fruition. It was as weakening as knowing that she was about to be made homeless, and that come the weekend she could throw away her house keys for all the use they would be to her.

By half past two, while appearing outwardly calm, Colly had become so het-up from going over and over everything in her head that she just could not take any more. Neither could she marry him, and that was that, and the sooner she told him the better. She would phone again—oh, grief, with his tight schedule he would be too busy to take phone calls.

That was when she noticed that she was not all that far away from the Livingstone building. At five to three she was pushing through the plate glass doors.

While she knew where Silas Livingstone's office was, there was a way of doing these things. And, anyhow, he might have someone in his office with him, which meant that she could not just bowl in there unannounced.

She went over to the desk. 'I'm Columbine Gillingham,' she told the receptionist. 'Is it convenient to see...' she got cold feet '...Ellen Rothwell?'

Her insides started to act up, and that was before the receptionist came off the phone to pleasantly say that Mrs Rothwell was expecting her. 'You know the way?'

Colly hoped that by the time she reached Ellen Rothwell's door she might have calmed down somewhat. But not a bit of it; she felt even more hot and bothered and was fast wishing that she had not come. She was recalling those steady dark blue eyes that had looked into hers—almost as if he could see into her soul.

I'm being fanciful, she scoffed. But her insides were still rampaging when she found Ellen Rothwell's door and went in.

'Silas isn't back yet, but if you'd like to take a seat he won't be long,' Ellen informed her pleasantly.

Colly thanked her, but felt more like standing up and pacing up and down than sitting. But she went and took a seat, realising as she did so that, while it was highly unlikely Silas would have confided in his PA any of this very private business, it looked very much as if—appointments with him being like gold dust—he must have mentioned that he was prepared to take calls from Columbine Gillingham, and that if she appeared personally he would fit her in with his busy schedule somehow.

Then the outer door opened, and while her heart leapt into her mouth it quieted down again when she saw it was not the man she had come to see. This man was about the same age as Silas, and about the same tall height. But that was where any likeness ended. He was sandy-haired, and where Silas had a strong, rather nice-shaped mouth, this man's mouth was weak—and that was before he opened it.

'Ellen, lovely girl—is my cousin in?' he wanted to know, his eyes skirting from her to make a meal of Colly.

'Not yet,' Ellen replied, but his attention was elsewhere as he turned his smile full beam on Colly.

'Are you here to see Silas?' he queried—and, before she could answer, 'Kit Summers,' he introduced himself, and held out his right hand.

It would have been churlish to ignore it. Colly shook hands with him—and wanted to pull her hand back when he held it over-long.

'What's a nice girl like you doing in a place like this?' Kit Summers asked flirtatiously.

Heaven help us! This man might be left to run the company! Colly caught Ellen doing an eye-roll to the ceiling, and felt a hysterical kind of laugh wanting to break loose.

Kit Summers was not at all put off that Colly did not answer, but, continuing to beam at her, suggested, 'Look, Silas might not be back for ages—why don't I take you for a cup of tea?'

Colly stared at him. This chinless wonder was married, yet by the look of it did not miss an opportunity to flirt. She was about to give him a cool, No, thank you, when Ellen Rothwell interceded.

'Have you the figures Silas wanted?' she enquired evenly.

That shook him sufficiently for him to take his eyes off Colly for a moment. 'Hell, was it today he wanted them? Strewth, I'd better be going. Don't tell him I was here,' he said. 'And deny any rumour you may have heard that I was on the golf course this morning!' With that he was gone.

Colly sat there feeling stunned and with her insides churning. Silas's cousin was a lightweight, and it showed. And if first impressions were anything to go by he was not fit to run any development company, much less an international one.

Then suddenly her mouth went dry. She heard sounds coming from the next-door office. If she wasn't very much mistaken, Silas was back.

She was not mistaken—the intercom buzzed into life. 'Has Kit been in?' Silas asked.

'Been and gone, I'm afraid,' his PA answered, and quickly, before he could enquire about any figures, 'Miss Gillingham is here to see you.'

The announcement was met with total silence. And, quite desperately wishing that she had written, or phoned, but certainly that she had not come in person, Colly went from hot to cold and to hot again. All at once there was movement on the other side of the door, and a moment later the door was opened and Silas Livingstone, tall, commanding, and the very opposite of his cousin, stood there.

He did not smile, or remind her that he had been going to give her a call tomorrow evening, but, 'Hello, Colly,' he said mildly, with his eyes fixed on hers as if he would read there what she had come in person to tell him.

Colly stood up. The time had arrived to give him the answer that would not wait until he telephoned tomorrow. He took a step back, so she should go first into his office, and following her in closed the door behind them, giving them all the privacy they needed.

CHAPTER THREE

'WHAT have you got to tell me?' Silas asked.

'I...' She was nervous; her voice got lost somewhere in her throat.

She moved more into the centre of the room, but, indicating one of the easy chairs, 'Come and sit over here,' Silas invited calmly. If he was aware of how mixed up inside she felt, he was not showing it.

With him towering over her, to sit across the room from him seemed a good idea. Colly went and took a seat—then found that Silas had no intention of going over to sit behind his desk when he came and took the easy chair opposite hers.

'I'm sorry to have intruded on your day.' She found her voice. 'I know how busy you are!'

If she had expected him to say that it did not matter she would have been in for a disappointment. For he said nothing of the sort, but, getting straight to the point, 'You couldn't wait until tomorrow to give me your answer?'

'My answer was no,' she replied promptly.

'On Friday.' He immediately got down to business. 'On Friday it was no. You've had time to think about it fully since then.'

She had thought of little else. 'My answer was still no this morning,' Colly answered. 'Only...'

'Only?' he took up when she hesitated.

'Only—well, to tell you the truth, I found myself weakening when this morning Nanette—um—mentioned—well, to be honest— This is extremely embarrassing for me!' she broke off to exclaim.

'You're doing well,' Silas stated calmly. 'Carry on.'

'Well, it would seem I soon won't have anywhere to live.'

'That "lady" wants you out?'

Colly coughed slightly. 'By the weekend,' she agreed, not missing that he did not seem to have much time for her 'lady' stepmother. 'I said this was embarrassing,' she mumbled. 'Anyhow, my trawl of just a few rental agencies has shown that I'm going to be hard put to it to find the rent.'

'So on that basis you decided, yes, you'd change your mind and agree to marry me?'

'No,' Colly denied. 'I'm being as honest with you as I know how,' she added quickly. 'My answer first thing this morning was still no,' she went on openly, explaining, 'When you and I are virtually strangers to each other, it goes against everything in me to allow you to, in effect, keep me while I undertake whatever training I need to make a career for myself.'

She paused for breath and looked at him. But he said nothing, just sat quietly listening—and assessing.

'Anyhow,' she continued, 'in the light of this morning's happenings—my imminent homelessness and inability to afford anywhere to live—I found I was weakening in my decision to—er—not take you up on your offer.' She took a shaky breath. 'So I thought I shouldn't wait until tomorrow to tell you, but tell you today. But I couldn't get you when I phoned earlier. Then I was close by, so I thought I'd better come and tell you in person.'

'Before you weakened further?' he suggested.

'Yes,' she replied. And hesitated again. Never had she felt so totally all over the place as she did then. 'But...'

'But?' Silas prompted when she seemed momentarily stuck to know how to go on.

'But—I've just met your cousin.'

Silas moved his head fractionally to one side, alert, interested. 'And?' he enquired.

'Oh, Silas,' she said in a rush, 'you can't possibly allow him to take over the company!'

Silas looked at her levelly for ageless seconds. Then, quietly, he let fall, 'You, Colly, have the power to stop him.'

She stared at him, her heart thundering. She felt she was teetering on the biggest decision of her life.

'Forget your pride at taking assistance from me,' he urged after some moments, 'and think of what you will be doing for me, and this company. I, in turn, will benefit far more than you,' he reminded her.

That made her feel a whole deal better. But it still did not make it right. 'Why me?' she asked as the question suddenly came to her. And, looking at him, seeing everything about him shrieking sex appeal, 'You must know any number of women who would agree to this?'

He did not deny it but gave her question a few seconds' thought before replying. 'You because you, like me, have a need, and we would be helping each other. And you, if I'm to be as honest as you, mainly because you don't want to marry me and would prefer any other way if you could find one.'

'Ah!' she exclaimed, as it suddenly dawned on her. 'Me because you know I won't get in your hair afterwards and try to make capital of it?'

He stared at her. 'Precisely,' he acknowledged, and with entire spontaneity they both burst out laughing. It was good to laugh with him—it lightened the serious atmosphere.

Then the intercom buzzed and Ellen Rothwell, apologising for the interruption, was informing him of telephone calls queuing up and reminding him of an appointment he had to keep.

Colly stood up. It seemed to her that she had intruded on his day for long enough. 'You still want to—um—do this?' she asked as Silas, on his feet too, looked down at her.

'Most definitely,' he replied, his eyes on her fine green eyes.

Colly took a long breath. She could hardly believe she was about to commit herself to marry this handsome virile man, but, 'You'd better say when,' she consented.

Silas did not take a moment to comprehend that she had just agreed to be his wife. Nor did he waste words, but stated, 'The sooner the better,' and, at once decisive, went over to his desk, wrote something on a piece of paper and returned to hand it to her. 'You'll want to have a look at your new home,' he said. 'We'll have matters to discuss too. I can be there around nine this evening. Is that all right with you?'

Grief, when she was committed she was committed, she realised. Silas was not hanging about. 'Fine,' she said faintly, and made for the door.

She left the Livingstone building in something of a daze. Had she just done what she thought she had? Had she just done what she had not intended to do? Was she, in effect, engaged to marry Silas Livingstone?

Over the following few hours her all-over-the-place feelings settled down. One way and another there had been quite an upheaval in her life lately. First her father had died. Then, before she could come to terms with his passing, she had learned that there was no way her father's wife was going to let her continue to live under the same roof. And now, Colly mused, she was going to have to come to terms with being— a wife!

Though not a proper wife, she hastily amended. She would meet Silas tonight and sort out any and all loose ends. They would no doubt agree on a wedding date, then it would be that half-hour in front of a registrar, and that should be it.

With so much whirling around in her head she only just remembered that she had promised to ring Rupert Thomas, who owned the art gallery where she helped out on Tuesdays.

'Tell me you're coming in tomorrow,' he pleaded. And,

prone to exaggeration, 'I missed you dreadfully when you didn't come in last Tuesday.'

Rupert was forty, and had been married twice but was currently single. He was a good friend. 'I'll come in tomorrow,' she agreed. 'How's business?'

'Terrible, terrible!' he replied, but it always was, according to Rupert, so there was nothing new there. They chatted for a few minutes, then Colly ended the call.

She supposed she should go and see about getting something to eat, but did not fancy another of Nanette's mean-spirited comments should she be around.

She did bump into her, though, when, in ample time to get to the address Silas had given her by nine, she left her room. 'Where are you going?' Nanette demanded.

In truth, Colly was finding her more than a little tedious, and was tempted to tell her to mind her own business. But politeness cost nothing, and this woman had brightened the last few years of her father's life—even if she had not stayed true to him.

'I'm going to take a look at an apartment,' she replied, and felt quite pleased to see that Nanette looked more taken aback by that than she would have done had she told her to mind her own business. But she was not taken aback for long, and was soon there with another of her spleenish remarks.

'I hope for your sake it will be vacant by Saturday!'

Saturday! Colly left her home unhappily aware it could no longer be called a home. She thought of her mother and could have wept. It had all been so different when she had been alive. So much love…

Colly put love out of her mind. She was getting married without love. Silas was too, and that suited her fine. Which reflection brought a previously unthought question to mind. Silas had said they would have matters to discuss. And he was right there!

Until now she had not thought there would be so very much

for them *to* discuss. But, for a start, what happened if one of them fell in love with someone? And how would they go on about a divorce? She supposed that that was the way their marriage would end—in divorce—with neither side battered or bruised by the experience. But what if Silas fell in love with someone and wanted out? What then?

Most oddly, she experienced a small niggle of impatience with the thought that he might fall in love with someone. Odd really was the word for it, she mused as she pulled up outside a newish-looking apartment block. She most certainly was not interested in him herself!

Colly was the first to arrive. She stayed in her car and observed the smart entrance to the building. It seemed incredible that she might soon be moving in here, but so far she liked what she saw.

A short while later a long sleek car pulled alongside, and as her heart suddenly missed a beat she recognised Silas Livingstone behind the steering-wheel so her insides joined in and did a churn.

Leaving her car, she went with him, waiting while he unlocked the entrance door. The apartment block was over three floors; the apartment owned by his grandfather was on the ground floor.

'It's lovely!' she exclaimed as Silas took her from room to room. It was small, as he had said, but only in that it consisted of just one bedroom, a sitting room-cum-dining room, a bathroom and a kitchen. All the rooms were otherwise spacious. Colly came from a very nice home herself, but had nothing to complain about in this her new home.

'Any of the furniture you can't live with can be put into storage,' Silas offered when they returned to the sitting room.

'Everything's fine,' she responded. Some of the furniture was antique, and beautiful, though there were some very pleasing modern pieces too.

'If you want to, bring some of your own furniture,' he suggested. 'I should like you to feel at home here.'

'That's kind of you,' Colly replied, smiling at him while thinking him most considerate. Without doubt the man had a great deal of charm. 'But I'm quite happy with the apartment the way it is.' She forbore to tell him that Nanette would probably call the police if she saw one stick of her inheritance making its way into any furniture van.

Silas took her at her word and handed the keys to the apartment over to her. 'Move in as soon as you like,' he instructed.

'You don't think we should stand in front of that registrar first?' she questioned, but could not deny that she felt pleased at this show of his trust in her.

'There seems little point in you spending a couple of weeks in some hotel when this place could benefit from someone living in it. Shall we sit down?' he suggested.

'I'm missing something?' she queried, confessing, 'Where does "hotel" come into it?'

'It doesn't,' he answered, and began to enlighten her into the working ways of his mind. 'Ellen has been able to shunt my diary around in order for me to have some time off to-morrow.'

'Yes?' Colly murmured, supposing that what he was talking about would become clearer.

'You're free tomorrow morning?' he asked.

'I promised Rupert I'd—'

'Rupert?' Silas cut in, his expression stern.

'It's not a problem,' she replied. 'Rupert owns the art gallery I help out in on Tuesdays. I said I'd be there tomorrow, but if I need to I can ring and cancel.'

'Cancel!' Silas instructed bluntly.

What happened to charm! 'Because...?' she queried stiffly.

'Because we both need to attend to make arrangements for the nuptials.'

'Oh!' she exclaimed, a little bit startled. She had already

formed an opinion that Silas Livingstone was a 'have it done by yesterday' kind of man. But—and she supposed she had not got around to thinking about it too much—she had rather thought their marriage would happen some time. By the sound of it he was keeping to that 'the sooner the better' comment. 'What time do you…?'

'I'll call for you at ten-twenty. You'll need either your birth certificate or your passport.'

'Er—I'll be ready. Um—when were you thinking of…?'

'Doing the deed?'

That was one way of putting it. 'You don't want to delay, by the sound of it?'

'No point,' he agreed. 'Though, since we apparently have to wait fifteen clear days after tomorrow, and a non-work day would suit me best, I'd suggest we marry two weeks on Saturday.' He looked at her questioningly.

'I've no objection to that,' she agreed faintly. His remark with regard to her not spending a couple of weeks in some hotel was starting to make sense. What he had been saying was that, since she would be without a roof over her head come the weekend, she might as well move in straight away rather than spend time in a hotel prior to their marriage.

'Good,' he said.

She started to feel a little panicky. 'This marriage…' she said in a rush. Though when she saw that she had his full attention had difficulty in continuing.

'This marriage?' he asked.

This was absurd. Spit it out, Colly, she fumed, irritated with herself. 'It wouldn't… I mean, I wouldn't have to—er—do anything—er—else?'

'Anything else?'

Oh, surely he wasn't that obtuse! For a moment she hated him that he was making her spell it out. 'Live with you—I mean.'

'You have your own apartment,' he replied urbanely, and she felt like boxing his ears.

'You said you occasionally spend a night here.' She dug her heels in stubbornly. She needed it all cut and dried now, and could not leave any question unanswered. 'And, while you may have given me a set of keys, I don't doubt that you still have a spare set.'

'True.' He did not deny it.

'Well…' She could feel herself going pink, but it had to be said. 'I wouldn't want anything—er—physical between—'

'You're blushing,' he interrupted, seeming fascinated at the tide of colour that flowed to her face.

And that annoyed her. 'I mean it!' she said stubbornly. 'I don't want a husband—' She broke off, looked at him, and everything suddenly righted itself in her head and settled. 'And you don't want a wife,' she ended, it being plain to her then that 'anything physical' was way off his agenda.

'You obviously needed to work that through,' he remarked casually.

She began to feel hot all over that she had ever brought the subject up. 'You're sure you need to do this?' she questioned hurriedly to cover her embarrassment. And, when he looked unsmiling at her, 'I mean—' she glanced from him and around the graciously appointed room '—I seem to be doing very well out of this.'

He nodded. 'Drastic circumstances call for drastic measures.' She had known that he would not be taking this 'drastic' action if he could find some other way out. And while drastic action was not very flattering to her, it was also fine by Colly. It was the same for her too. Her impending homelessness, her joblessness, her inability to earn sufficient to make her independent, made drastic action the only way possible for her too. 'I know my father,' Silas went on. 'Unless he was absolutely certain that my grandfather meant every word rather than cause me disquiet my father would have kept their conversation strictly to himself. You,' Silas said, looking straight into her green eyes, 'are my insurance.'

She looked away, uncertain how she felt about that. But considering all that had gone on, all that would go on, she realised that now was not the time to get picky because, not dressing it up, her intended was telling it as it was. Her intended! Oh, heavens!

Then she recalled how earlier that evening she had pondered on the question of their divorce. But when she looked at him it was to see he was taking out a card and handing it to her. 'My home address and phone number,' he informed her. 'I cannot see a situation arising when you'd need either, but—'

'I can,' she interrupted.

'You can?' He was looking stern again, whether because he did not care to be interrupted or because he was not too happy that she might have a complication that would see her wanting to phone him every five minutes, Colly could not tell.

'We've discussed the legal aspects of—um—what we're about.' Ridiculously, the words 'our marriage' stuck in her throat. 'But what about at the end of it?'

'End of it?'

There he was again, making her spell it out! 'Divorce. What—?'

His expression darkened. 'They'll be no divorce!' Silas stated harshly.

'No divorce?' It was her turn to echo his words this time.

Silas shook his head. 'My grandfather has very old-fashioned views on the sanctity of marriage. To him divorce is a dirty word. I have no idea of how he intends to word his new will, but I can be certain, from what I know of him, that there will be a clause in there somewhere to the effect that should any such marriage I have contracted end in divorce prior to his demise—Kit's marriage too for that matter—then the other cousin inherits the shares.'

'He's got you pretty well sewn up, hasn't he?' she commented.

'He has,' Silas admitted. 'And I resent it.'

'Er—you're not going to tell him you're married—when you are?'

'Hell, no!' Silas said forthrightly.

'Because you're—aggrieved with him?'

Silas shook his head slightly, though owned, 'A bit of that, perhaps, but mainly because he would want to meet my bride.'

'Oh, grief. I hadn't thought of that!' Colly exclaimed, mentally backing away fast from the very idea.

Silas favoured her with one of his rare smiles. 'While I know little about you, Colly, other than using my instincts, from what I *do* know about you I'd say you won't be telling anyone of our marriage either.'

'For my part, there's no one who needs to know,' she answered. He really had quite a superb mouth when he smiled. 'Um—shall we keep it between our two selves, then?' she asked. Good heavens, what was the matter with her? Abruptly she switched her gaze from his mouth to his eyes.

He gave a small nod. 'I may have to give my father some kind of hint that he has no need to worry. But you can rely absolutely on my discretion.'

'I'm sure,' she murmured. And from nowhere the words came rushing from her mouth. 'What if we marry but you fall in love with someone?' She had his full attention, and felt a touch awkward, but rushed on, 'What if you want to marry someone else?'

'I won't.'

'How do you know?' she exclaimed, not a little amazed by the confidence in his statement.

'She'd have to be more than a bit extra-special for me to

think so much of her that I'd be prepared to divorce you and so risk my inheritance going to my cousin.'

'You don't know anyone—er—that extra-special?' Colly found herself enquiring.

His mouth quirked upwards. 'She doesn't exist,' he returned pleasantly.

Colly mulled that over for a moment, then concluded, 'I'll marry you, because it suits us both, but I think we should have some sort of time limit.'

'You think you may fall in love and want to marry elsewhere?' he demanded, every bit as though he thought she was deceiving him—and that was before they started.

'No!' she denied hotly, her green eyes sparking at this hint he thought she might not be being absolutely honest with him. 'I've told you. I'm more interested in making a career for myself than in matrimony. I just—just need to cover all bases, all eventualities, that's all. And I—I think it's best to have these matters sorted out now, rather than on the registry office steps in a couple of weeks' time.' She ran out of breath, and owned to not being too enamoured that he had turned her question about him and his love-life around and fired it back at her.

Silas stared at her, his gaze on the spirited look of her, his glance slipping briefly to her mouth before he fixed on her eyes once more. Then he told her seriously, 'I'm afraid I cannot agree to any time limit in the length of our marriage,' explaining, 'To do so would be to speculate on my grandfather's demise, and that is abhorrent to me.'

'Oh, I couldn't agree more,' she said impulsively, suddenly wondering why it had been important to her anyway—Silas had more or less stated that he would not want to divorce during his grandfather's remaining years. 'I'm sorry,' she apologised. 'It was insensitive of me to push the issue.'

Silas looked at her contemplatively. 'Do you know?' he began a moment later. 'I do believe I'm getting me a very nice wife.' Colly could only look at him, but at once she realised that there was absolutely nothing intimate or anything for her to worry about in his remark when, in the same breath, and as if to take anything personal out of what he had said, he followed up with, 'You'll be dating, I expect, during our marriage?'

Her lips twitched. 'You're saying that you won't?' she bounced back at him. And, impossibly, they both laughed.

'That seems to be everything, I think,' he said a few seconds later. 'Unless there's anything else you'd like to ask?' She shook her head, finding that she enjoyed sharing laughter with him. 'Then I'll just show you where to garage your car, and we'll be off.'

Silas Livingstone was in her head the whole of the way home. He was still there when she went in and searched around in the drawer where personal papers were kept for her birth certificate.

'What are you nosing around in here for?' Nanette asked on coming into the study and seeing her with a rolled up piece of paper in her hand. 'What have you got there?'

'Nothing that belongs to you,' Colly replied evenly. And she realised that she did not have to put up with this woman for very much longer, that, in fact, now that she already had the keys to her new abode in her bag, she could move out tomorrow if she cared to. 'Since I shall soon be living elsewhere, I'm taking papers personal to me with me.' With that she escaped to her room.

Colly was about to go to the drawing room to wait and watch for Silas the next morning when she belatedly remembered that she had not telephoned Rupert. She was not surprised she had forgotten. The fact that she was going to marry Silas Livingstone two weeks on Saturday had kept her thoughts elsewhere. But Rupert would have expected her at the gallery twenty minutes ago.

She was on the hall phone to Rupert when her housecoated

stepmother floated past on her way to fix herself a cup of coffee. But while Colly was attempting to console Rupert— all 'his' women were against him, apparently, and his latest lady-love had last night dumped him—the doorbell rang.

'I'm sorry about that, Rupert,' Colly said, wanting to get to the front door before Nanette got there first. 'But I'll...'

Too late. Nanette was there. Colly heard her delighted coo of surprise, and was not listening at all to what Rupert was bending her ear with as Nanette invited Silas into the house.

'All I said to her,' Rupert was complaining, 'was that...'

Nanette took Silas into the drawing room and closed the door.

'I'm sorry, Rupert, I really must go. I have some business to attend to, but it shouldn't take me too long.'

'You liked her, didn't you?'

Meriel? He must be referring to his dumper. 'She was very nice. Look, Rupert, I must dash. I'm sorry I didn't call earlier, but...'

It seemed to be all of five minutes before she was able to put down the phone and hurry to the elegant drawing room, where Nanette was acting out the sad, but available, widow.

'Here you are,' she trilled sweetly as Silas got to his feet. 'You forgot to mention that Silas was calling.'

Colly ignored the question in her voice. 'I almost forgot to ring Rupert too,' she answered lightly. And, turning to Silas, 'I'm sorry to have kept you waiting.'

'You're sure I can't tempt you to coffee?' Nanette enquired of him.

'Thank you, no,' he replied urbanely. 'Ready, Colly?'

Nanette gave her a frosty look that said she would be asking questions later, and Silas escorted Colly out to his car. 'I was ready on time,' Colly commented as they crossed the drive to his car.

'And then you remembered Rupert?' Silas filled in.

'I've—er—had other things on my mind,' she mumbled as he held the passenger door open for her.

'Will you mind very much having to leave here?' he asked, looking back at the substantial house with its fine furnishings.

'I…' she began, then shook her head. 'It—isn't home any more.' And was aghast that her voice should unexpectedly go all wobbly.

To her surprise Silas stretched out a hand and touched her arm in a moment of sympathy. 'It will get better,' he comforted softly.

She was suddenly ashamed of herself. 'It has already,' she said brightly, and got into his car, telling herself she must guard against such weak moments, but starting to like this man she was going to marry. She liked especially this more sensitive side of him.

Their business at the register office was dealt with without fuss, and in no time they were back in his car and Silas was returning her to the only home she had ever known but which on Saturday she would leave for ever.

'I can't think of any reason for you to contact me but you have my phone numbers should you find a need,' he said, when at her home she went to open the car door. 'Just a moment.' He halted her, and took a ring-sizer from the glove compartment. 'Better get the size right.'

A tingle shot through her as he took her hand to get the measure of her wedding finger. 'I can use my mother's wedding ring,' she said hurriedly.

'Are you calling me a cheapskate?' he teased—and she found she liked that about him as well, his teasing, just as if he sensed she was suddenly uptight and, when she was nothing to him, easing her through it.

She got out of the car to find that he had stepped out too and was coming round to her. 'I'll—um—see you two weeks on Saturday,' she said by way of parting.

He nodded. 'Move into the apartment as soon as you're ready,' he suggested, and that was it. He was gone.

Nanette was avid to know how she knew Silas Livingstone and what he was doing calling for her, and where had they gone?

'He's in the engineering business like my father,' Colly replied offhandedly, and decided Nanette could make of that what she would because it was all she was getting.

Colly then went to the gallery and listened to Rupert going on and on—and on—about the ingratitude of Meriel. When he had for the moment paused to seek fresh charges to lay against Meriel's door, Colly told him that she was moving to an apartment.

'I don't blame you!' he exclaimed, obviously having no idea that she had been left penniless and of the opinion that she could afford to rent or buy. 'What your father saw in that Nanette creature, I shall never know!' he dramatised, having met her once, fancied his chance, but received short shrift when Nanette had her eyes set on more lucrative game.

Colly went home late that afternoon and began putting her belongings together. She moved to her new home on Friday— and was not bitterly disappointed that Nanette had taken herself off clothes shopping and was not there to say goodbye to. Colly left her house keys on the hall table—and went quickly.

The weeks leading up to her wedding went in turns fast and then slowly, fast and then slowly. She was soon settled into her new abode, and liked where she was living and its surrounds, but experienced a feeling of edginess. Perhaps it was through the speed with which everything had happened and was happening. She owned to a few panicky moments too whenever she thought—that day creeping nearer and nearer, galloping nearer and nearer sometimes—of how she was going to marry the tall, distinguished-looking Silas

Livingstone. Sometimes it seemed more like a dream than reality.

She did not find any reason to contact him. Though would not have minded some reassuring word. Reassuring? Get a grip, Colly, she lectured herself, you're twenty-three—and life is going to get better. It already had. While she still missed her father, grouch that he had been a lot of the time, at least she didn't have to spend time being picked on by his widow.

When, with two days to go before she married Silas, the telephone in the apartment rang, Colly nearly jumped out of her skin. For several fearful seconds she was too alarmed to answer it. What if it were Silas's grandfather, the owner of the apartment?

Common sense settled that one. Why on earth would he ring what he thought was an empty apartment? She picked up the phone, said a tentative, 'Hello,' ready to say, Wrong number, if indeed it were Grandfather Livingstone. Then with utter relief she heard Silas's voice and realised, by the same token as she had his home number, he had the number of the phone in the apartment should he find a need to contact her.

'Any problems?' he enquired evenly.

'Not one. But I'm glad you phoned,' she said impulsively—and wished she hadn't because, while Silas politely waited for her to tell him why she was so glad, she started to feel a little foolish. 'It doesn't seen real somehow,' she explained lamely.

'Trust me. It's real,' he answered, but there was a smile in his voice.

'I know,' she said, and felt better. 'Any problems your end?' She batted his enquiry back at him.

'None that Saturday won't see secured,' he replied easily, and, getting down to the purpose of his call, 'I'm about to transfer some funds into your account,' he informed her, going matter-of-factly on when she felt too awkward to have anything to say, 'Can you get me your bank details? I'll hang on if you need to find you account number.'

Wanting to tell him not to bother with that now, that he could see to all that once they were married, Colly, realising he was too busy to want to call her again on this issue, obediently went to find her cheque-book—unused of late.

But, having given him the details he required, she just could not hold back from saying hurriedly, 'There's no rush! If you don't want to—'

'I want to,' he cut in, that smile in his voice again. And, about to ring off, 'Does your bank know your new address?' he enquired.

She hadn't given that a thought. 'I'll do it tomorrow,' she replied.

'Then I'll see you on Saturday,' he said.

'I won't be late,' she replied as evenly as she could manage.

Nor was she late. January had given way to February: not the most exciting month of the year. She had wanted to buy something new to be married in, and had then lectured herself that this was more a half-hour in front of a registrar than a marriage. In any event, funds would not run to anything new—even though she supposed that by now Silas would have seen to it that her bank balance was the healthiest it had ever been.

But that money was not for some extravagant clothes-buying session, but as a base to get her started on some sort of career training—Colly knew she would never ask him for more, for the subsequent top-ups he had mentioned. So she went out to her car dressed in a pale yellow biscuit-coloured suit she'd had for some while but which still looked good.

She was some minutes early arriving at the register office, and was relieved to see that Silas was already there. He came towards her, and seemed to like what he saw. For her part she had to admire the way his suit fitted him to perfection, the way he effortlessly wore clothes.

'You look lovely,' he said by way of greeting, and if he'd had any idea how sorely her confidence needed a booster just then, he could not have said anything better.

She wanted to say something bright such as, You're not looking so bad yourself, but the nerves that had kept her sleepless last night were attacking again, and all she could say was a husky, 'Thank you.'

She had spent a tormented night having last-minute doubts. And, having arrived at the register office, having decided to go through with it, had done nothing to dispel her nerves. But if Silas had picked up something of how she was feeling he did not refer to it, but stated calmly, 'I've roped in a couple of witnesses,' and, looking steadily into her worried green eyes, 'Ready to make a fresh start?' he asked.

And suddenly his words, his steady look, made everything fall into place. She knew why he was marrying her—to secure the future of the company he headed. And, by marrying him, she in turn was securing her own future, securing for herself that fresh start she so sorely needed.

And, looking at him, she liked what she saw, and just had to beam a smile at him. 'Let's do it,' she agreed.

Not so long after that she stood beside him in front of the registrar and, in front of the witnesses he had found, took him as her lawful wedded husband. The strange feel of his wedding ring on her marriage finger brought home to her that, as Silas was her lawful wedded husband, she was his lawful wedded wife.

Emotion gripped her at the end of the ceremony when, by tradition, the marriage certificate was handed to her as her property. Colly turned to Silas and, the certificate of marriage being all that he was interested in, she handed it over to him. He took it from her, looked down at her, and smiled his wonderful smile.

Her insides were already having a merry time within her. But when he bent and gently placed his lips on hers her heart joined in the general mêlée. 'Thank you, Colly,' he murmured.

He had kissed her! This was not a love-match but—Silas had kissed her. A second later, however, and she was realising that they were not alone. Aside from the registrar, they had witnesses. Should questions be asked at some later date as to the romance or otherwise of their wedding, then any witness could state that there had been 'romance in the air'.

Colly swiftly got her head back together. For goodness' sake, anyone would think she wanted his kisses! She gave him a smile of her own—two could play at that game—and waited nicely while he thanked their witnesses—she gathered he had settled any financial arrangements in advance—and, Saturday a busy day for weddings, apparently, they left so that the registrar could go and check through details with the next couple.

From the register office Silas escorted Colly to where she had parked her car. And suddenly it all seemed just a little too much. She looked at him as they stood by her car. She had married him, this man. This man was her husband, yet it was unlikely that after today their paths would ever cross again. She did not know what to do, whether to shake hands or just get into her car and drive off. She certainly wasn't going to kiss him. She opted to unlock her car.

'Would you like lunch?' he asked abruptly, almost as if the question had been dragged from him.

She opened the driver's door. Oh, my word, her insides were on the march again. 'You haven't time,' she replied—this man never had a minute to breathe.

'Today I could find time,' he replied.

She didn't thank him. He obviously felt he should give her lunch rather than allow her to just drive off. She shook her head. 'I only signed up for a half-hour,' she told him, and saw his lips twitch the moment before he stood back to allow her to get into the driver's seat. Her lips twitched too. 'Bye,' she said and, looking at him, saw that they were both grinning.

'Bye—wife,' he said, and as she got into her car and he closed the door he began walking away.

She passed him, drove by him; they both waved. Somehow she had never imagined that her wedding day would be like this. That the last she would see of her husband on her wedding day would be through the rear-view mirror of her car, the distance between them getting further and further apart.

She remembered the happy way they had grinned at each other. Yet suddenly she could have burst into tears, and had to acknowledge that one Silas Livingstone was having a most peculiar effect on her.

CHAPTER FOUR

By Monday, having removed her wedding ring, though unable to remove the lingering memory of the touch of her husband's lips on hers, Colly had got herself back together again. By then she was scorning any such notion that her emotions were in any way affected by Silas Livingstone. Still the same, an involuntary smile came to her mouth that she was married to the man, his name was now her name and, if she cared to, she could use it. Which, of course, she did not care to. Though she could not resist saying 'Colly Livingstone' out loud to hear what it sounded like.

She abruptly turned her back on such nonsense and reached for the telephone book. A short while later she had taken the first steps towards enrolling for a foundation course.

Disappointingly, although an application form would be put in the post, to be then followed up by an interview, she had been told that it was unlikely she would be able to start before the September term.

Which meant, since pride reared and made it impossible to use Silas's money while she spent the next six or seven months in idleness, that she must get a job. Now what? She decided against secretarial—she still blushed when she thought of her nerve in going for that secretarial interview.

Only then did it come to her that it was perhaps from some inner instinct that had warned she would not get that secretarial job that she had not previously told Rupert that she had been looking for work. But when she went to the gallery on Tuesday she felt that to be fair to him she ought to warn him that her circumstances were a little different from what they had been and that she was going to have to look for temporary full-time paid employment.

Rupert, as ever with his head in the clouds, took that 'temporary' to mean that the lawyers were dragging their feet over settling her father's estate and that they had temporarily frozen all assets.

'I expect your dear stepmama will make sure she gets her grasping fingers on some of it.' Unasked, he gave his opinion. But straight away was thinking of his loss rather than that of his unpaid helper as it dawned on him that he stood to be without his Tuesday helper. 'You can't leave!' he exclaimed. 'You're so good with the customers! And who else can I trust to look after this place when I'm out buying?'

'You'll find someone,' Colly tried to reassure him.

'I'll have to *pay* them!' he replied. But, his eyes lighting up, 'I'll pay you!' he decided. Though, as ever covering his back, 'It won't be very much, of course. But at least it will be enough for you to be able to keep your head above water.'

This was Rupert in full skinflint mode. But, in considering his offer, Colly realised since she had no work experience other than housekeeping, plus the little bit of work she did for him, that in those circumstances to work for him full time in a poorly paid job was quite a good deal.

'You do know that there's a minimum wage allowed by law?' she thought to remind him. She just could not afford to work for nothing. And, while Rupert was always moaning about his lack of funds, it was she who mainly kept his books, so she knew that financially he was doing quite nicely, thank you.

'You drive a hard bargain, Miss Gillingham,' he grumbled, for the look of it, but stuck out his hand to shake on the deal.

Mrs Livingstone, she mentally corrected him, and had to smile at how ridiculous she was being. Thankfully Rupert thought she was smiling at the done deal. They formally shook hands.

The very next day she received a statement from her bank showing that her account was in excess of ten thousand pounds in credit. Even though she knew about it, she still felt shocked to see it there in black and white. But, as she started to adjust to the fact that Silas had paid ten thousand pounds into her bank, she still knew that she would continue to work full time for Rupert and use Silas's money only when she had to. It still did not feel right to take his money—even if it had been all part of their bargain.

Colly, her application for the foundation course posted off, was two weeks into her paid employment, and was busy in the small office, when someone called at the gallery to collect a picture his mother had bought. 'I'm double parked,' she heard him tell Rupert. There was only one picture awaiting collection. She picked up the carefully wrapped painting and, thinking to save him a second or two, took it out to him.

'Mr Andrews?' she enquired—and discovered that Mr Andrews was not in that much of a hurry.

'Tony Andrews,' he introduced himself. And, obviously liking what he saw, 'Miss...? Mrs...?' he enquired. 'I'm sorry, I don't know your name.'

What could she do? She was a paid member of staff. Besides which, there was no mystery about her name. 'Colly Gillingham,' she supplied. 'Um, they're a bit hot on double parking around here.'

'I shall return,' he promised, and went.

He did return too—to ask her out. Colly was unsure, and reflected for a moment that neither she nor the man she had married had placed any restriction on dating, but she said no. Tony Andrews was undeterred and returned a few days later to ask again, with the same result.

Then on Tuesday of the following week something astonishing occurred. She was working at the gallery when the door opened and her father's old friend, Henry Warren, came in.

'Uncle Henry!' Colly cried, and, feeling quite choked suddenly, she went speedily over to him and was given a fatherly hug. 'How was the holiday…?' she began.

'We came home on Saturday. But it wasn't until last night that I went to my club.' He looked at her sadly. 'I was so sorry to hear about Joseph.'

'It must have been a great shock for you,' she sympathised, realising that someone at his club would have told him of his friend's death.

'Last night was my night for shocks. I went straight round to see you, only to hear from a gloating Nanette that you'd moved out without leaving a forwarding address. Luckily I was able to remember your father mentioning something one time about you having a little job in this gallery.' A smile came to his lined face then, to be joined by a look of utmost satisfaction as he added, 'The dear Nanette wasn't gloating after I'd told her what I had to tell her.'

'You told her off about something?' Colly asked, feeling a little mystified.

'That creature thought she was sitting pretty,' he replied. 'It was my happy duty to inform her that, shortly before I went on holiday, your father contacted me and made a new will.'

'My father…'

'Your father had started to realise that, apart from being very unfair to you, he had been something of an old fool.'

Colly just stared at him. 'Good heavens!' she said faintly.

'As you probably know, he was so besotted with Nanette that he was blind to anything else. But by and by he began to come to his senses and to be appalled by what he had done—the way he had willed his affairs. He came to the club, seeking me out.'

'But—you're not his legal representative.'

Henry Warren smiled again. 'Poor Joseph. He was too embarrassed at realising his foolishness to go back to the firm he had always dealt with. I drew up his fresh will in secret.'

He paused, then announced, 'He left everything equally between the two of you.'

Colly looked at him disbelievingly. 'My father left me...' She could not continue.

'He left you half of everything. The house, his money, his shares.'

That word 'shares' brought Silas to mind, but she tried to concentrate on what Henry Warren was saying. 'Er—come into the office. I'll make us some coffee,' she said, trying to gather her scattered wits. But coffee was forgotten when, in the office, she asked, 'It's—legal, this new will?'

Henry Warren gave her a reproachful look. 'You should know better than to ask such a thing,' he said with a smile. 'I made certain it is totally watertight,' he assured her. 'It goes without saying that neither your father nor I had any idea that he would so soon depart this life.' He halted for a solemn moment, as if remembering his friend, before going on. 'But I know he would want me to look after your interests, Colly. To that end I have taken steps to have all your father's assets frozen.'

Colly confessed herself little short of stunned. 'Does Nanette know—about everything being frozen?'

'If she doesn't, she soon will,' he replied cheerfully.

Colly was having difficulty taking it all in, her mind a jumble. 'Coffee,' she remembered, but more from some kind of need to do something practical.

It was over coffee that he asked for her new address. She did not want to lie to him, but did not feel able to tell him the facts of her marriage to Silas. Their marriage was private, secret between her and Silas, so she simply gave Henry Warren her new address and phone number.

He assumed she was renting the apartment and jovially told her, 'You'll be well able to afford to buy somewhere to live now. For that matter you'll have funds enough to buy out

Nanette's share of the house, should you want to move back in there.'

'There's that much?'

'Oh, yes.' He nodded. 'Given that that woman is going to take half of everything, you'll be quite moderately wealthy once the estate is settled.'

Several things struck Colly at one and the same time then. One was that she was happier living in Silas's grandfather's apartment than she had been living with her father and his second wife. And two, she did not want to go back to that house. Life after her mother's death had been pretty bleak— she only then realised just how bleak. But more important than anything was the realisation that she had money of her own now. She did not have to use Silas's money!

'I've no idea how long it will take for my father's affairs to be wound up,' she commented, and just had to ask, 'Is there any chance I might have…?' She felt embarrassed asking.

'Of course.' Henry Warren, as if aware of her embarrassment, cut in at once. 'I don't doubt that Nanette has managed to talk your father's previous executors into allowing her to draw something on account.'

Colly went home that night with her head in a spin from these latest developments. But a week later she was in a position to take action on a matter that had troubled her from the beginning. She had accepted Silas's ten thousand pounds because of the deal she had made with him. But she had never been truly comfortable about taking his money; it had never seemed right. It had gnawed away at her from time to time, even before Uncle Henry had called at the gallery last week. Since his visit the fact that she had taken that money had started to become untenable.

That night she wrote to Silas, telling him of her father's lawyer friend Henry Warren, and how he had returned from holiday and had come to the art gallery with the astonishing news of her father's newest will. She wrote that, while she was extremely grateful to Silas for his support when she had so sorely needed it, she no longer had need of his money. She enclosed her cheque for ten thousand pounds. Added to that she stated how she loved living in the apartment and how, if he was agreeable, she would like to stay on as a rent-paying tenant. She wished him well, and signed it 'Colly'.

She posted her letter on her way to the gallery on Wednesday morning. She had addressed it to Silas's apartment, about twenty minutes away by car from where she was living. With any luck, if he replied straight away—say he received her letter and cheque tomorrow—she might have a response from him in the post by Saturday.

His response came sooner than that, and in person. She had finished her evening meal on Thursday and was tidying up in the kitchen when someone knocked on her door. She realised at once that it must be one of the other occupants in the building, otherwise her caller would have buzzed from the outside door so that she could let them in.

So far, apart from exchanging a morning or evening greeting with her fellow apartment dwellers, she had not had anything to do with her neighbours. Ready to be friendly, she went to the door, opened it and stared in quite some surprise. Somehow she had fully expected a written response.

'You've got a key to the outer door?' she said witlessly.

'We established that,' Silas replied, his eyes going over her trim shape in trousers and light sweater. 'And to this door— but I thought you'd prefer me to knock rather than walk straight in.'

She smiled at him, realising with more surprise just how very pleased to see him she was. 'Come in,' she invited. And, as he crossed the threshold, 'You received my letter?'

'I did,' he confirmed. But did not seem too ecstatic about it. In fact he sounded quite tough as he demanded, 'You're saying you want to divorce?'

Colly stared at him, her jaw dropping. 'When did I say that?' she gasped, startled.

'You wrote in terms of ending our agreement!'

'No, I didn't!' she retorted, facing him on the sitting room carpet. 'I merely mentioned that I've money of my own now. And, to be blunt, I have never felt very comfortable about taking yours.'

'You agreed—'

'I know. I know!' she butted in, feeling all het-up suddenly—and who wouldn't with those dark blue eyes glittering at her? 'But I'm no longer in need of your financial support.'

'But you otherwise intend to keep to our agreement?' he demanded.

'Of course,' she replied, and, a grin starting to break because he looked so fierce, 'It's sheer bliss being married to you.'

'We seldom, if ever, meet,' he commented and, his eyes on her sparking eyes, his lips twitched. 'The perfect marriage,' he endorsed.

Her heart gave a peculiar kind of leap. 'But since we have met—and you are here,' she took up, striving to be sensible, 'is it all right for me to stay on here now that...?'

'I find it offensive you need to ask!' he replied curtly.

Pardon me for breathing! 'Will you allow me to pay rent, then?' she tried.

His answer was sharp and unequivocal. 'Not a chance!' He chopped her off before she could finish.

'At least think about it!' she bridled.

'It doesn't need thinking about. We made a contract, you and I. Paying rent never came into it.'

'But I didn't know then—'

'No!' he said, the matter closed as far as he was concerned, his tone brooking no argument, and, before she could try anyway, 'You're comfortable here?'

'Who wouldn't be? I love it here.'

'Good.'

'And that's your last word on the subject?' she protested.

'It is!' he returned brusquely.

That did not please her. She turned and led the way to the door. 'I would have offered you coffee,' she informed him shortly, but opened the door so he would know he could die of thirst before she would make him a drink.

'I would have refused it!' he answered in kind. And she just did not know what it was about the wretched man—she just had to laugh.

'Bye, Silas,' she bade him.

She saw his glance go to her laughing mouth—and she felt her knees go weak when he smiled. 'Bye,' he said, and added, 'Wife.' And, before striding away, he bent down and lightly kissed her.

He was much in her head after that. She quite liked his light kisses, she discovered. Not that there had been so many of them. Only two, in fact. One possibly to seal the deal of their marriage. And the other probably to pay her back for not making him a coffee. It was, she owned, quite a nice punishment.

She then scorned such a ridiculous notion. But recalling his 'You're saying you want to divorce?' and his 'You wrote in terms of ending our agreement,' she then realised the reason he had called in person in preference to writing. It was their agreement he was concerned about. He needed to establish, now that she no longer needed his help, exactly where he stood with their agreement and their marital state, with regard to his future concerns in connection with his grandfather. Why else would he have called in person for goodness' sake? She had invited his visit by breaking their unwritten 'no communication' clause and writing to him.

Colly decided the next day that she was thinking far too much about Silas, and determined not to think about him any more. To that end she accepted a date with Tony Andrews.

Tony was in public relations, and was quite amusing with his various anecdotes, but she was not sorry when the evening was over.

He tried amorously to kiss her—much too amorously. She had been kissed before, but discovered a sudden aversion to being kissed—amorously or any other way. 'Goodnight, Tony,' she bade him, pushing him away. For goodness' sake!

'Never on a first date, huh?'

Nor second or third. She went indoors half wishing she had not gone out with him—and wondered how mixed up was that. Then saw that she had gone out on a date more because she thought she should than because she wanted to.

Tony asked her out again, several times, but she told him she didn't consider it a very good idea. 'I'll behave myself,' he promised. She told him she would think about it.

Colly still found herself drifting off to think about Silas. It was two weeks now since she had last seen him. She wished he would allow her to pay rent, but had to accept that free use of the apartment was part of their agreement. She had to accept also that Silas was the kind of man who disliked being indebted. In the circumstances, she supposed she must be grateful that he had accepted her breaking their agreement to the extent of returning that ten thousand pounds.

Only the very next day she discovered, when another bank statement arrived, that Silas had not accepted it. Her bank balance was ten thousand pounds better off than it should have been. Silas had not cashed her cheque!

Feeling winded, Colly stared at the figures on her statement as if to magic the removal of that money. But, no, it was over two weeks ago now. She rang her bank; perhaps the transaction was in the pipeline. It was not.

She heaved a sigh. She did not feel like writing to Silas a second time, and went to the gallery wondering what, if anything, she could do about it.

'I'm just popping out for an hour,' Rupert said when he came in.

'You've only just got here!' She made the effort to rib him. There was a new woman on his scene.

'Busy, busy, busy!' he chortled, and was off.

They were not particularly busy, as it happened, and, after doing a few chores, Colly, with Silas in her head, went and made some coffee and took up the newspaper Rupert had discarded before going out.

She was several pages into it when, with alarm shooting through her, she saw a possible reason for why Silas had not banked her cheque. He had been out of the country. He had been in the tropics on business—but had returned home and was now gravely ill.

Shocked, stunned, and with fear in her heart, she read on. Apparently Silas had been struck down with some tropical bug and was hospitalised in an isolation ward. It gave the name of the hospital. She felt dizzy with fear—and had to ring the hospital. As did everyone else, it seemed—press included. She learned nothing.

Colly just could not settle, and when Rupert returned she had her car keys at the ready. 'I have to go out,' she told him without preamble, and guessed he could see that she was going to go whether he gave permission or not.

'Will you be long?' was all he asked.

'I don't know.'

'Take as long as you need,' he replied, and she was grateful to him that he did not ask questions but simply held up her coat for her.

Never had she felt so churned up as she did on that drive to the hospital. She afterwards supposed that it must have been sheer determination that got her as far as the doors of the isolation unit.

'Can I help?' enquired the stern-looking nurse who blocked her from going any further.

'Silas Livingstone?' Colly queried. 'How is he?'

'He's doing well,' the nurse replied, her eyes taking in the look of strain about Colly, her ashen face.

Tears of relief spurted to Colly's eyes. 'He's getting better?' she asked huskily.

'He's doing well.' And, a smile thawing the nurse's stern look, 'And you are?'

'Colly Gillingham,' Colly replied. 'He really is doing well?' She had to be sure.

'Are you and Mr Livingstone—close?' the nurse wanted to know before she would disclose more.

Married was close. 'Yes,' Colly answered.

And then learned that they had been able to sort out the bug and, while Silas would continue to be hospitalised, once that morning's test results were through they were hoping to release him from the isolation unit to another part of the hospital. Colly let go a tremendous sigh and a little colour started to return to her cheeks.

'Thank you,' she said quietly, and turned away.

'Would you like to see him for a few minutes?'

Colly turned swiftly about. She knew she should say no. Against that, though, she experienced a tremendous need to see for herself that he was better than that 'gravely ill' that had scared the daylights out of her.

'May I?'

'You'll have to wear a gown and all the gear,' the nurse warned. It was a small price to pay.

To be swamped by a cotton gown, wearing a cap and face mask, was insignificant to Colly when, with the nurse showing the way, she entered the isolation room.

Colly's heart turned over to see Silas, his eyes closed, propped up on pillows. 'A visitor for you, Mr Livingstone,' the nurse announced—and stayed to make sure that they really were known to each other.

Colly went forward. Silas opened his eyes as she reached

his bed and just stared at her. He looked washed out, she thought, but, realising that dressed as she was she could have been just about anybody, 'It's Colly,' she told him.

'Who else do I know with such fabulous green eyes?' he returned. Her green eyes were about the only part of her visible.

The nurse was convinced. She went from the room.

'Sorry to intrude on your illness,' Colly apologised primly, much relieved to see Silas looking better than she had anticipated. 'I saw a report in the paper that you'd picked up some tropical bug and…' she racked her brains for a reason '…and I thought I'd better come and check that I'm not a widow.'

She had no idea where those words had come from. But, to her delight, Silas thought her comment funny, and as he leaned against his pillows—washed out, exhausted as he seemed to be—he laughed, he actually laughed—and Colly accepted at that moment that she was heart and soul in love with him.

'I'd better be going,' she said, wanting to stay and to stay and never to leave him. 'Your nurse said I should visit for only a few minutes. You should be resting.'

'I've done nothing but rest since I got here.'

'You'll be on your feet in no time,' she encouraged.

'Why did you come?' he asked, but his eyelids had started to droop. Colly thought it was time to tiptoe out of there.

She did not go to see him again. She wanted to. Days trickled by, and some days she did not know how she held back from going to the hospital to see him. But to go to see him again was just not on. The only requirement in their agreement was that she stand with him in front of a registrar and make the appropriate responses. No way could she go to the hospital a second time and risk Silas again asking, 'Why did you come?'

So she stayed away, though she fretted about what sort of progress he was making. She daily scanned the paper for some sort of progress report, but saw nothing in the pages of print about him.

Then suddenly, early on Friday evening—a week since she had been to see him—her telephone rang. Silas, she thought! But that was because Silas was always in her head. Both Uncle Henry and Rupert also had her address and this phone number.

'Hello,' she said down the instrument. It was neither Henry Warren nor Rupert Thomas.

'I've a bit of a problem!' She would know that voice anywhere. Silas! Her heart started to thunder.

'Where are you?' she asked, striving hard to take the urgency out of her voice.

'For the moment, still in hospital.'

'For the moment?' Her concern antennae went into action. 'They say you can go home?'

'I'm going home,' Silas replied.

There was a subtle difference between 'They say' and 'I'm going'. Colly picked up on it. 'You're signing yourself out, aren't you?' she questioned, trying to hold down her feelings of anxiety.

'In the morning.'

Don't panic. Stay calm. 'Are you well enough to leave?' she enquired, amazed she could sound so even, when she was inwardly a ferment of disquiet.

'I'm fed up with this illness, not foolhardy about it,' he responded. 'I've had enough. Another day in here and I'll be climbing the walls. The problem is,' he went on, getting down to the reason for his call, 'while I've promised my father I won't return to the office until my physician gives me the nod, my mother has threatened to come and nurse me if I *do* sign myself out. Unless,' he added, 'I can do something about it.'

'That sounds reasonable to me,' Colly said with a smile.

'You don't know my mother. She's wonderful,' he said,

'but memory of her attempts to mollycoddle me at the first childhood sniffle makes me know she'll fuss and cosset me to death if I let her an inch over my doorstep. She'll want to take my temperature every five minutes and feed me every ten.'

'Perhaps you'd better stay where you are,' Colly said sweetly.

'Not a chance!' he fired unhesitatingly back, then paused and said evenly, 'Actually, it was my mother who gave me the answer.'

'What answer?' Colly fell straight in.

And she was sure she could hear a smile in his voice because of it, as he began to reveal, 'It was while I was resisting all arguments that she move in, with my mother insisting that she was the natural choice for someone to come and "watch over" me—that on its own was threatening enough—that when she attempted to settle her argument with the words "It's not as if you have a wife to look after you" I had an idea.'

'You didn't tell her you had a wife?' Colly exclaimed in shock.

'I wasn't *that* panicked!' Charming! 'I just thought, if you're not busy with anything else just now—purely to keep my mother off my back—you might care to come and stay for a night or two. Naturally, without question, you'd have your own room. I just...' His voice seemed to fade, and she guessed he was far from back to his full strength yet.

She loved him too much to put him through further strain. It did not take any thinking about. 'I'll come and see you at the hospital at ten tomorrow,' she said decisively. And, bossily, 'Now go to sleep.'

'Yes, Mother,' he responded meekly—but Colly just knew that his lips were twitching.

She sat for ageless minutes after his call, just thinking about him. She supposed that for a man who was always up to his eyes in work, always so very busy, that to be so incarcerated would truly drive him up the wall. Particularly now that he had started to mend and was no longer as gravely ill as he had been.

Colly had no idea of what was involved in 'watching over' him, but, while obviously not back to top form yet, he must be feeling well enough to leave hospital. And if Silas needed someone to be there so that he was not in his home alone overnight, or during the day, for that matter, then Colly knew that she wanted that someone to be her and no one else.

CHAPTER FIVE

WITH Silas her first priority, Colly rang Rupert at his home that Friday night and asked if he'd mind if they reverted to her previous hours of work.

'Ah, your money's come through and you no longer need to relieve me of my hard-earned cash,' he replied.

'My heart bleeds,' she joked with him. 'Will that be all right?'

'I shall miss you,' he answered, adding soulfully, 'Nobody makes coffee like you.'

'I'll be there to make you some next Tuesday,' she said, and rang off.

When she left the apartment the following morning Colly was carrying an overnight bag. That to stay with Silas and keep any eye on him as he recovered had never been part of their agreement was neither here nor there. She loved him, was in love with him, and if he was in trouble—in this case still unwell—with him was where she wanted to be.

He was already dressed when she arrived at the hospital, and was sitting in a wooden-armed chair. Colly's heart went out to him—he looked far from well.

'You've lost weight!' she observed when, impatient to be off, he got to his feet.

He adopted a kind of sardonic look of pathos. 'I've been poorly,' he sighed.

As ever, he made her laugh. But she still was not too happy about him leaving hospital. 'Are you sure you should be—?' she began.

'I've already had this lecture,' he cut in sharply.

'You just wait until I get you home!' she threatened

toughly, and turned away when she saw him trying to suppress an involuntary laugh of his own. 'Sit down again while I go and check up on your medicines,' she instructed, and went quickly to find someone in charge.

Armed with a mental list of dos and don'ts, Colly went back to Silas. 'Now?' he questioned, rising from his chair. He *had* lost weight Colly fretted, but clamped her lips shut so not to make another comment. She must keep her anxieties to herself.

Stubbornly he walked unaided to her car—it was quite some way. It was a cold day; she turned up the heater. Silas was asleep five minutes later.

She knew his address, and fortunately found it without too much trouble. Silas stirred as they arrived outside the stately building where he had his apartment. 'It's impossible to park around here,' he said, and was alert as he directed her to where his garage and the parking area was.

From there she took charge and drove round to the front of the building again. 'You go in while I park,' she suggested.

That he did not argue showed her that he was not feeling as strong as he might have thought he was. Colly parked her car, grabbed her overnight bag from the boot, and hurried to him. He had left the door ajar; she went in.

'Not in bed yet?' she enquired mildly, on finding him seated in a beautiful high-ceilinged drawing room.

'You don't know how good it is to be back,' he replied.

'Coffee?' she suggested, and found her way to the kitchen while she wondered on the best approach to get him to go to bed. She did not want to argue with him, or say anything in the least contentious that might see him pulling the other way. But in bed seemed the best place for him.

She returned to the drawing room with a tray of coffee, handed him a cup and took hers to the seat opposite. 'You'll probably want to rest in bed after you've drunk that.' She tried the power of suggestion.

'Why? What have you put in it?'

She wanted to laugh—and hit him at one and the same time. Hints, she saw, were going to be a waste of time. 'You may be out of hospital, but you still need your bedrest.'

He gave her a disgusted look but forbore to tell her that she was worse than his mother. 'How have you been?' he enquired instead.

'Me? Fine!' she replied, not caring to be the subject under discussion. 'Better than you, I'd say.' She attempted to put the conversation back where she wanted it.

'If you need any help winding up your father's estate, my people will—'

'Thanks for the offer, but everything's going smoothly,' she butted in. 'Nanette wants to sell the house and I've no objection.'

'She has your present address?'

'No, but I've been working full time at the gallery and Uncle Henry pops in whenever there's anything new I need to know. I told you about Henry Warren, my father's friend?'

Silas did not answer her, but questioned something else she had just said. 'You're working full time? I thought you only helped out there one day a week?'

'I did,' she agreed. 'But when I discovered that the foundation course I'm interested in doesn't start until September I realised I'd better find some paid employment, so I—'

'We agreed I was to fund you!' Silas cut her off, sounding annoyed.

'It didn't seem right that I should sit idly back and use your money while waiting for my course to start,' she explained. 'But, since I'm not qualified to do anything in particular, I told Rupert I need to find paid employment, and he said he'd put me on his payroll.'

Silas still did not look overjoyed. 'So you've had to ask for time off in order to spend two or three days here?'

She shook her head. 'With my father's new will my financial position has changed. I rang Rupert last night and told him I'd like to go back to our old arrangement.'

What she expected Silas to reply she could not have said, but a kind of grunt was what she did get, coupled with something that sounded very much like, 'You're too proud by half!'

'Look who's talking!' she retorted. 'You're dead on your feet but won't give in!' And, guessing from the set of his jaw that she was going to get nowhere with him with that attitude, 'Come on, Silas, give me a break.' And, when he looked obstinately back at her, 'I shall have to pop to the shops in a little while. I shall feel much happier in my head if I know you're lying down regaining your strength.'

'What have you to "pop to the shops" for?' he wanted to know.

'You have to eat. If I'm to cook meals for you—'

'You don't have to cook my meals!' he objected—and Colly stared at him, and started to get cross.'

'Look here, Livingstone. I've given up my job—not much of a job, I admit, but all I'm likely to get until I'm trained—to come here and keep an eye on you. But if I'm not allowed to cajole you to bed, and nor am I allowed to see to it that you take proper nourishment, then would you please mind telling me just what exactly I am doing here?'

'You're here to answer the phone when my mother rings—which she is going to any minute now, if I'm not mistaken. And—' he gave her a wry look '—you shouldn't talk to me like that. I've not been well.'

Laugh or hit him? She was tempted. Laughter won. She turned away so he should not see. Though she soon sobered, to turn back and quickly ask, 'Your mother knows I'm here? Who I am? I mean, that we—um—got married?'

'Hell, no! If she knew I'd married she'd be round here to meet you quicker than that. I just told her a kind, close friend, who had nothing else on at the moment, was coming to stay for a few days.'

And that annoyed Colly. Though, as she was well aware, jealousy was the root cause. 'You have many "kind, close" women-friends with nothing else on at the moment?' she asked shortly.

He shrugged. 'None that I'd care to give that sort of advantage.'

Colly thought about his answer and realised he was meaning that, because he knew she had no ulterior motive in answering his SOS, he could trust her not to want to get too domesticated with him. The fact that they were already married to each other, but only married for expediency and no other reason, made her, in his eyes, nothing of a threat.

'I think—I'm not sure—but I think you've just paid me a compliment.'

He did not tell her whether he had or he hadn't, but informed her, 'Mrs Varley was here most of yesterday. She—'

'Mrs Varley?' Colly interrupted him. He might be physically weakened, but she knew she would have to stay on her toes to mentally keep up with him.

'She's the good soul who comes and housekeeps five mornings a week. When she's not cleaning, washing or ironing, she cooks. She also shops. She said when I rang that she'd leave a pie ready for today's dinner.'

'Presumably I'm allowed to heat it up?'

The phone rang before she received any answer. 'Tell my mother I look well and that—'

'I'm expected to answer your phone?'

'She'll be here jet-propelled if it goes unanswered,' he hinted, not moving.

'Go to bed.' Colly openly blackmailed him.

'I could always tell her we're married, I suppose.' He bounced her blackmail with blackmail of his own. Colly decided not to risk it.

She went over to the insistent telephone and picked it up. 'Hello?' she said, feeling more than a touch nervous.

'Hello,' answered a warm-sounding voice. 'I'm Paula Livingstone, Silas's mother,' she introduced herself. 'And you're—Colly?'

'That's right,' Colly replied.

'You got that son of mine home all right? How does he seem? He won't tell me if I ask him, so I just have to use your eyes.'

Colly cast a glance over at him. 'He seems much improved from the last time I saw him.' She thought that was a nice safe answer.

Only to realise she had invited more questions and no small speculation when Paula Livingstone enquired, 'You saw Silas when he was in hospital?'

Somehow Colly did not feel she could lie to her. 'Only for a short while—when he was in the isolation unit.' Colly saw Silas give a 'tut-tut' kind of look at what she had just said. She turned her back on him.

'They let you see him? Oh, that is nice,' Paula Livingstone remarked warmly. 'They said that only family members were allowed in when...'

Oh, heavens. Colly realised that Silas had straight away seen this development in the split second she had owned to seeing him in that particular department. 'I saw him on his last day there—I believe Silas was transferred out of the isolation unit soon after.' She had to turn and take another look at him—he was shaking his head from side to side. Colly felt a laugh bubbling up, and wondered if she was growing slightly hysterical. 'We're just having a cup of coffee, then Silas is going to go to bed for a little while,' she volunteered.

'Oh, good. I'm so glad you're there with him,' Paula Livingstone said genuinely.

'Would you like to speak with him?'

'No, no. He'll only accuse me of being a fusspot. I'd come

over in person, but he always did have a rigid independent streak. I naturally dropped everything when Silas was so ill. Which means I'm way behind with my committee work. But if you need me for any reason—no matter how small—I'll be there. Just give me a call.'

Colly came away from the telephone having warmed to Silas's mother but hoping that she would not have to speak to her again. It was too fraught with holes for her to fall into. 'I didn't handle that too brilliantly, did I?' she said to Silas unhappily.

'You did well,' he answered.

Colly knew that she had not done well. 'I'm no good at subterfuge,' she remarked. 'All I've done now is let your mother believe I'm almost as close to you as family.'

'We're still not getting divorced,' he countered, pulling a face that made her laugh.

'Oh, shut up,' she ordered. 'And, if you don't want to make a liar of me, go to bed.'

Silas gave her a long steady look, but to her amazement he got up and, without another word, went from the room. That alone told her that he was more tired and used up that he would ever admit to.

Moving quietly so as not to disturb him, Colly stacked their cups and saucers onto the tray and took them to the kitchen. As silently as she could she washed the dishes and investigated the cupboards. He would need a light meal of some sort shortly.

Having taken a look in the fridge and the freezer, she saw that Mrs Varley had been extremely busy. There was enough food there to last through a siege. Colly prepared some vegetables for the evening meal, and began to wonder where her room would be.

She felt a little hesitant to investigate, but would not mind knowing where she was to sleep that night. Taking her overnight bag with her, she went along the hall. There were several doors to choose from.

Anticipating that one of them would be the door to Silas's room, she tapped lightly on the wood panels of the first door and quietly opened it. It was a bedroom. Silas's bedroom.

He was neither asleep nor in bed, but, fully clothed apart from his shoes, he was lying on top of the bedcovers reading. He lowered his book and glanced at her over the top of it.

'Sorry to bother you,' she apologised, feeling suddenly all flustered—how very dear to her he was. 'But I was wondering—looking for my room.'

'I should have shown you,' he said, and before she could stop him he was off the bed and coming over to her.

'I'll find it!' she protested. 'Just—'

'I'm not *totally* debilitated!' he butted in harshly, and led the way along the hall to a room at the end. 'This do?' he questioned brusquely, opening the door and allowing her to enter first.

For a few seconds Colly was in two minds about staying at all. She was doing *him* a favour, not the other way round! Then she looked at him and realised that he hated being ill, hated being weakened, and hated like blazes having to ask anyone for help. And her heart went out to him.

So she smiled at him. 'You're a touchy brute, Livingstone,' she told him sweetly. 'And this,' she said, going in and looking round, 'is a lovely room.' A grunt was her answer as he left to return to his room.

After unpacking her bag Colly went to the kitchen. She decided on a ham omelette with some salad, and would very much have liked to take it to Silas on a tray—she doubted very much that he possessed a bed-tray. But, in view of his scratchiness not so long ago, she decided to treat him as he wished to be treated. She laid two places at the kitchen table and, when everything was ready, went to his room.

'I've laid the table in the kitchen. Lunch is ready when you are.' She turned about and went back to the kitchen. When less than thirty seconds later he joined her, she felt he had been nicely brought up not to let the cook's efforts go to waste.

He had eaten only half his omelette, though, when he put down his knife and fork. 'Sorry,' he apologised. He plainly could eat no more.

Colly smiled at him because she had to. 'You're forgiven,' she assured him. And, apologising in turn, 'I'll try to be more understanding,' she added.

And loved him the more when, his mouth tweaking at the corners, he told her, 'My wife really doesn't understand me.' She had to smile again, but could not deny a small glow to hear him call her his wife.

With lunch out of the way, she saw to it that he had his medication. She thought he was looking a trifle worn again, and began to wonder if she was the best person to look after him. She was having difficulty in being objective where he was concerned.

She was relieved when he took himself off to his room, and, guessing he had no intention of getting into bed, felt that at least just by lying on top of the covers he would be resting.

He wandered into the kitchen while she was cooking the evening meal—one of Mrs Varley's chicken and mushroom pies, with duchesse potatoes, broccoli and glazed carrots.

Colly saw that his appetite had not fully recovered, in that there was quite some of the meal left, but she guessed he had enjoyed what he had eaten when he asked, 'Where did you learn to cook?'

'Given that dinner was mainly Mrs Varley's efforts, my cooking skills came from what I think is called "on the job training",' Colly answered.

'You had no formal training?'

She shook her head. Their housekeeper had walked out the week before Colly had been due to leave school. She left school one day and was housekeeper the next. 'There's sponge pudding if…'

'Thanks, no,' he refused. Colly did not push it. 'It's hot in here. I think I'll go to my room,' he volunteered.

It did not seem unduly hot to her. 'You're very hot?' she asked, trying not to look as concerned as she felt.

'Hot, cold—it's all part of the fever territory. It will pass,' he said confidently, and left the table.

Colly busied herself clearing up after he had gone, but determined to keep a watch on him whether he liked it or not. To that end she went to his room at just after ten. He was in bed this time, and although propped up on pillows had his eyes closed. His shoulders and arms were uncovered, so she had to assume that he either slept without pyjamas or that he was still feeling hot.

'I've brought you some water. You may be thirsty in the night,' she said pleasantly as he opened his eyes. 'I was just about to make myself a drink—can I get you anything? Tea? Not coffee. You'll never sleep if—'

'Come and talk to me,' he interrupted her.

'You're bored?'

'And some!'

'Poor love,' she said softly, the endearment slipping out before she could stop it. She was going to have to watch that. 'Still feeling hot?' she asked in her best professional manner.

'Not now,' he replied, and, as if trying to remember that he was the host here, 'Have you everything you need?' he asked. 'If you…'

'I've absolutely everything I need,' she told him hurriedly and, when it looked as though he might sit up and take charge, she went quickly to the side of the bed and sat down on it beside him. 'I believe you're looking better already,' she said encouragingly. 'If you could bear to rest as much as possible over the next few days—' She broke off when he gave her a look that said she was adding to his boredom. 'Right,' she said snappily, 'I'll relieve you of my company!'

'What did I say?' he protested.

She looked at him, and loved him so much. 'Try to get some sleep,' she said gently, and as she went to stand up she felt such a welter of compassion for this strong man who had been flattened by some tropical bug that she just could not hold back on the urge to bend over and kiss him.

The feel of his lips beneath hers brought her rapidly to her senses—what on earth did she think she was doing? She straightened quickly, and was about to wish him an abrupt goodnight—only he found his voice first.

'Was that part of the nursing package?' he asked, his eyes solemnly on hers.

Oh, help! 'Just pretend I'm your mother,' Colly brought out from an awkward, embarrassed nowhere.

'My imagination isn't that good!'

'Goodnight,' she bade him crisply, and went from his room, knowing that she was never, ever going to do that again.

Indeed, away from him, she could hardly credit that she had done such a thing. He had not asked her to kiss him, and certainly did not want or need her kisses. Though, having worked herself up into something of a state, Colly recalled how, unasked, he had kissed her—twice. And her het-up world righted itself. It wasn't his sole prerogative to go around kissing folk! Still the same, she would not be doing it again in a hurry.

Colly was awake several times in the night, and having to hold down the urge to go and check on Silas. Although he was mainly recovered from the more serious effects of the illness that had befallen him, he was still prey—to a much lesser degree—to attacks of hot and cold as the fever petered its unfriendly way out.

But she found it impossible to stay in bed beyond five the next morning, and got out of bed. Wrapping her cotton robe about her as she went, she could no longer hold down the urge to go and check on Silas.

She snicked on the hall light and went to his door. Just in case he was sleeping soundly she decided against tapping on his door, but, making no noise, slowly opened it. She stood in the doorway, but even with the light behind her she could make out little. She went further into the room.

Silas was lying on his back with his bare chest free of his duvet. All too clearly he had been hot again in the night. She stood looking down at him and wanted to place a hand on his forehead to gauge his temperature. But he was sleeping peacefully and she did not wish to disturb him.

Denying her need to pull the duvet up and over his shoulders, Colly turned away. Then, just as she reached the door, 'If you're making tea...?' an all-male voice hinted, addressing her back.

Laughter bubbled up inside her, but she did not turn around. Dratted man. He had been awake the whole time she had been looking down at him. She carried on walking—kitchenwards.

Silas was sitting up in bed with his bedside lamp on when she returned. 'Sleep well?' she asked lightly, handing him the tea he had requested.

'I was about to ask you the same question,' he responded.

'Very well,' she replied.

'You normally get up at five in the morning?'

'"Normal" disappeared when I collected you from the hospital yesterday.'

'Am I such a trial?' he asked seriously.

Looking at him, she had to smile. 'Not when you do as you're told.' She tried for a stern note—and failed.

'I'm famous for my biddable ways,' he blatantly lied.

Colly gave him a sceptical look. 'You're going to have breakfast in bed?' She challenged his protest, but could see the idea had absolutely no appeal.

'Must I?'

She folded. 'Oh, Silas. You're trying so hard.'

'Does that mean I don't have to?'

They breakfasted at seven, in the kitchen. At half past seven the telephone rang. 'My mother,' Silas stated, not needing second sight, apparently.

'She'll want to speak to you,' Colly replied.

'I know,' he accepted, and went to take the call.

A couple of hours later word seemed to have got around that he was now out of hospital, and he appeared to spend the rest of the day taking telephone calls.

He spoke to his father too, and also his cousin Kit. And, for all he may have promised his father that he would not return to his office before his physician advised that he could, and for all it was Sunday, it did not prevent Silas from having long and involved business conversations with his PA and also some of his directors when they rang to wish him well.

But at the end of that day, when Colly took a jug of water to his room, she felt that Silas was looking very much better than he had. She guessed that the stimulus of talking over complicated work issues was partly responsible.

'You've had a good day today,' she commented as she visually checked him over. He had recently showered and was sitting robe-clad against his pillows. 'But you won't overdo it tomorrow, after I've gone?' she dared.

Instead of agreeing that he would take care, 'Gone?' he demanded. 'Where are you going?'

Colly stared at him in surprise, her heart hurrying up its beat. It sounded for all the world as though he did not want her to leave! Logic, cold icy logic, hit that notion squarely on the head. He may not want her to leave, but only because if she was not there his mother might drop everything and come and fuss over him.

'You asked me to stay for a night or two,' she reminded him. 'Tonight will be my second night.'

'Have I been such a dreadful patient?' he asked.

'Well, given that you go your own way, regardless of anything I say, you have taken your medication when you should, so...'

'Stay another night?'

Willingly. 'You're just scared your mother will come and take over and make you eat your greens,' Colly managed to jibe.

'Please?' he asked nicely. Then, frowning, 'You're seeing someone tomorrow?' he demanded. 'You've a date and—?'

'Just because your love-life's out of bounds just now...' Colly began, and then gave him a smile of some charm, pleased by the thought that he was not physically up to— um—'tom-catting' just now. 'I suppose I could cancel my arrangement,' she conceded, there being no arrangement, and knowing she would not have to so much as lift the phone.

His frown cleared. 'You really should put your husband first, Mrs Livingstone,' he replied, his charm swamping hers.

Her heart lifted to be so addressed. 'Goodnight,' she said shortly—and went to her room almost dancing. He had called her Mrs Livingstone, and she was to have an extra day with him.

Her normal sleep patterns went haywire in her caring for him, and Colly was up again at five the next morning and going to check on him. He appeared to be sleeping peacefully, but she had been fooled before. 'Tea?' she asked, her voice barely above a whisper.

'Please,' he answered, but did not open his eyes.

That day followed a slightly different pattern from the previous day, in that although they again breakfasted in the kitchen, Paula Livingstone left it until seven-forty-five before she rang. Colly tackled the breakfast dishes, but Silas had not closed the door, and she could hear his side of the conversation.

'I'm all right!' she heard him repeat. 'There's absolutely no need... Yes... But... Fine, I'll see you tomorrow.'

'Your mother's visiting tomorrow?' Colly guessed when he returned to the kitchen.

'I should have known better than to argue,' he said, and looked so glum Colly burst out laughing. She was not laughing a moment later, though, when Silas smiled too. 'My mother is looking forward to meeting you,' he mentioned pleasantly.

'No way!'

'You'll like her,' he promised.

It was clear, despite his objections to the threat of being cosseted, that Silas loved his mother dearly. 'I'm sure I would,' Colly replied. 'She was lovely when I spoke to her on the phone. But I've already told you—I'm no good at subterfuge. In my efforts not to reveal the truth about us, I'd only go and say something I shouldn't. I just know I would. And anyway—' Colly began to slow down from her first flush of panic '—you can't want me to meet her. Ours is a secret— um—marriage.'

'True,' he replied. 'Though events we could not have foreseen have rather overtaken us.'

'You couldn't help being ill.' She found she was defending him.

'True again,' he responded. 'Though perhaps I shouldn't have asked you to come and collect me from the hospital.' He paused, his look thoughtful as he suggested, 'But perhaps you started it when—entirely unexpectedly—you decided to come to the hospital and pay me a visit.'

Steady, Colly. She was ready to panic again. By no chance did she want him speculating on why she had taken it into her head to do so. 'From that exaggerated newspaper report I thought you were gasping your last,' she trotted out cheerfully.

What he would have answered was lost when they were both alerted by a ring at the doorbell. 'Mrs Varley, come to "do",' Silas supplied at Colly's startled look. And, as Mrs

Varley used her own key to let herself in, a minute later Silas was introducing them. Mrs Varley was anxious to know how he was, and Silas told her he was all but recovered, adding, 'I'll make myself scarce.' A second later he was on his way to his bedroom.

'Is there anything I can help you with?' Colly asked Mrs Varley. The apartment looked immaculate as it was, but she could hardly sit around idle while the other woman set to.

'I have my own system that I like to keep to, thank you just the same.' Mrs Varley refused her offer cheerfully—and Colly wandered back to her room.

With her room tidy, and feeling uncomfortable at the idea of sitting doing nothing while a woman some thirty years her senior wielded a vacuum cleaner, Colly surveyed her options. She could sit twiddling her thumbs where she was, or alternatively she could go and sit with Silas in his room. He had complained the night before last about being bored, tempted a small voice. Against that, he had a telephone in his room. If yesterday were anything to go by, he would most likely be relieving his boredom by conducting some business.

Realising that he would not thank her for interrupting the smooth grinding cogs of industry, Colly saw her only option was to busy herself elsewhere.

Donning her car coat, she picked up her shoulder-bag—and paused. Her wedding ring was in her purse. She took it out, knowing she had no right to it. But—and she knew she was being weak—she just had to try it on one last time.

She looked at it on her hand and felt so emotional just then that she knew she needed to be away from the apartment for a short while. Taking the ring off, she left her room, found Mrs Varley and, after chatting for a minute or two, told her she would be gone about an hour or so. Then Colly went to impart the same information to Silas.

He was just putting the phone down, after either making or receiving a call when she went in. But, on noticing she was dressed for the outdoors, and before she could say a word, 'Where are you going?' he demanded.

'We need some salad things.'

'Mrs Varley can go out for any shopping!'

'Mrs Varley has enough to do!' Colly answered. 'Though if you ask her nicely I'm sure she'll make you a coffee when she has hers.'

He wasn't having that. 'I'll come with you,' he stated categorically.

'No, you won't!' Colly returned swiftly. And, ignoring the thrust of his chin that she thought she could tell him what to do, 'Mrs Varley says it's bitterly cold out—and you're still suffering extremes of temperature. You need to stay in the same environment.'

'Who told you that?' he questioned belligerently.

'Nobody had to tell me,' she replied, and, with a superior look, 'It's just something that women know. Now,' she went on tartly, 'is there anything I can get you while I'm out? Anything—' She broke off, then, eyeing him fixedly. 'Any cheques you would like me to pay into your bank?' She refused to look away—he did not bat a guilty eyelid. 'You *do* intend to bank that cheque I sent you, I hope?' she challenged knowing she'd want to thump him if he dared to ask what cheque.

He did not ask. But made her cross just the same when he bluntly retorted, 'I don't consider I should. We made a bargain, you and I—that money was part of it.'

'Agreed,' she said, purely because she could not deny it. 'But I have money of my own now, and I don't feel comfortable about taking yours.'

His look said tough, and that was before he forthrightly told her, 'Likewise! To take your money makes it too one-sided.' She opened her mouth to argue, but he went steam-rollering on, 'I have that piece of paper I need, that marriage certificate, that insurance. You have nothing. And that puts me under an obligation—and I don't like it!'

'And you called me proud!' she erupted. Then, remembering how very ill he had been, and how he still needed to take care, she relented to say softly, 'Have you forgotten what you did for me when I was so not knowing where to turn? Have you forgotten that I'm living in a lovely apartment, totally rent-free?'

'I've forgotten nothing,' he grunted.

And her patience ran out. 'Oh, you're impossible!' she snapped, and, digging her hand into her pocket she pulled out the wedding ring. 'Here,' she hissed, 'have this!'

'What is it?' he wanted to know.

She came close to braining him. 'It went with the "I will" bit!' she retorted—though could not recall those two words featuring in their marriage ceremony. 'I always intended to give it back to you. I just didn't think it seemly to do so on the register office steps.'

He took it from her. 'What am I supposed to do with it?' he rapped harshly.

She looked at him and wanted to box his ears. 'Keep it— as a memento of the good times!' she flew, then turned her back on him and marched to the door.

She heard his short bark of laughter—she had caught his sense of humour. Oddly, as she let herself out from the apartment, she realised that she had a grin on her face. She loved him so much. Even arguing with the wretched man made her feel alive!

Knowing that Mrs Varley was in the apartment, Colly stayed away for nearly two hours. Mrs Varley would make him coffee and anything else he might require. For herself, Colly knew she was getting too close to him. While she loved him, and wanted to be near him, she at the same time felt nervous about that closeness.

She supposed, as Silas had said, she had started the whole

thing rolling by going to see him in hospital that day. But to be with him was not part of their agreement, and, while it had been his idea that she come and stay, she could not help but feel that he might start to regret having asked her once his health was back to normal. Once he was back to his full strength, she had a feeling that he was going to dislike very much the situation she had instigated by that hospital visit.

When Colly returned to the apartment she felt calmer. It had done her good to get away for a short while—even if she'd had to make a determined effort to keep from returning. And while she intended to quietly savour every moment she spent with Silas, she also knew that she would not see him again after tomorrow. Tomorrow, before Paula Livingstone arrived, she would leave.

Since she had no key to the apartment, Colly rang the door-bell. Mrs Varley let her in and, after a few minutes spent in friendly chat, returned to her chores. Colly took her bits of shopping into the kitchen and, despite her strictures on keeping her distance from Silas, had to give in to an overwhelming need to see him.

She looked in at the drawing room on her way to seek him out in his bedroom. But he was in neither room. 'I'll come with you,' he'd said when she had told him she was going out. Oh, surely he had not gone out on his own! Trying not to panic, Colly went looking for him.

She found him in a room she had not been in before—it was a study. He was *working*! 'What do you think you're doing?' she demanded.

He looked at her—and grinned. Actually grinned. Did not look shame-faced, but *actually* grinned. Her fierce expression amused him, apparently. 'You wouldn't let me go out,' he replied innocently—a man who would do exactly as he wanted without bothering to ask her permission, thank you. 'I didn't think you'd mind if I found something to occupy myself with while you were gone.'

Colly calmed down, outwardly. 'Does that mean you intend to go and rest somewhere now?' she enquired evenly.

'My father called just after you left,' he ignored her question to announce unexpectedly. And, while she was getting over her surprise, 'He was sorry he missed you.'

Colly was not sorry. One way and another Silas's family were closing in. True, Silas had been extremely ill and was still recovering. Which meant that they must have been exceedingly alarmed and had more or less lived at the hospital until he had turned the corner, as it were. There was no way that they were not going to keep a check on his progress now.

'You said I was out?'

'I told him you went out looking for a lettuce—and might be some while.'

Her lips twitched at his hint that if it had taken her two hours to run some salad to earth, then it must be some pretty special salad. 'You didn't tell him anything else?'

Silas shook his head. 'What we have is personal to us, Colly.'

Her heart turned over at how wonderful that sounded, even though she knew full well that the only thing personal to them was their secret marriage. And in any event, while she instinctively knew that Silas would never lie to his father, Silas did not want anything more personal between them than those facts on that marriage certificate.

She turned away when the phone rang. She had an idea she would be wasting her time were she to insist that he rest. He was in the thick of business before she left his study.

And, in her view, he paid the price for not resting. Mrs Varley left at lunch-time. But Silas did not have any appetite for lunch. Colly took him some soup—in his study. He was not hungry at dinner-time either. Though he did insist on joining Colly at the dinner table.

'Why don't you go to bed?' she suggested when she saw he had eaten all that he was going to eat.

He looked drained, but even so she was sure he was about to say no. Worryingly, after a minute or so, he got up from the table.

He was in bed when Colly went in a short while later. He was not reading, but was just lying there. She grew more worried. 'As head nurse, is there anything I should know?' she asked lightly.

'I'll let you know,' he replied, and closed his eyes. Colly went quietly from his room.

But she could not settle. She felt marginally less worried when she heard plumbing sounds that indicated he was taking a shower. Still the same, she could not resist taking another look at him before she retired for the night. She tiptoed into his room. He had switched his light off and appeared to be asleep. She silently retreated.

She showered and got into bed—but she was awake at one, and awake at two. When the clock said three and she was still awake Colly gave in. It was no good. She just knew that she would get no rest until she had been to check on Silas.

Calling herself all sorts of a fool, she still the same got out of bed, slipped on her cotton wrap and, unable to deny the instinct that propelled her, went silently along the hall and, as silently, opened the door to his room. And at the sight that met her eyes she was never more glad that she did.

His bedside lamp was on and Silas was huddled up in bed—shivering. 'You're supposed to be asleep!' he admonished when he saw her.

She hurried into the room, not knowing what to do for the best. 'Where do you keep your hot-water bottles?' she asked, reaching him and pulling the duvet up closer around him.

'Don't have any,' he responded, his body shaking with cold.

That figured. 'I'll be back in a minute.'

'Don't you dare go calling out a doctor!' he instructed

shortly. And, when she stared at him obstinately, 'This is nothing to the attacks I had in hospital.'

That made her feel better, but only marginally. 'I'll just go and turn the heating up,' she said, and went looking for controls. Discovering that the system was programmed to shut down overnight, she switched it on full belt and then hurried to her room to grab up the duvet from her bed.

Back in his room, she wrapped the duvet around him. 'I'll just go and make you a warm drink,' she told him.

'A brandy would be good.'

'I'm unsure,' she answered. 'It might clash with your medication.' And, guessing he would probably gag if she made him some hot milk, 'I'll make some tea.'

She was still undecided about whether or not to call out a doctor, but decided to leave it a half-hour to see if Silas's shivering got worse. But in any case, after she took the tea into him she had no intention of leaving him.

She eyed his silk robe at the bottom of the bed, but didn't think there would be very much heat obtained were she able to get the robe around him. 'Sit up and drink this,' she said, and, first placing the tea down, she pulled her duvet closer around him.

In fact she still had an arm about his shaking form as he took a few swigs of tea, wanted no more, and leaned back against her.

'Put your arm in and try to get some sleep,' she urged gently.

He obediently put his arm under the covers, but more she suspected because he was cold than because she had told him to. 'You must sleep too,' he answered.

'I will—soon,' she replied, and, half sitting, half leaning on him, she secured the covers up and around him once more. 'Try to relax,' she murmured, realising he was tensing against the cold of his fever.

'Keep me warm,' he mumbled, and moved over so she should get closer to him.

It did not require any thinking about. Silas was her first priority, her only priority. She stretched out beside him on top of the covers, her head on the pillows, close to his head. 'You'll be all right soon,' she whispered softly.

'Don't get cold,' he mumbled, and said nothing more, but snuggled against her as though seeking her warmth.

And Colly lay against him, her arms around him. A few minutes later and she was of the view that she should be ringing a doctor or the hospital he had been in. A few minutes after that, though, and she thought his shivering had started to subside.

When another ten minutes had passed and, while Silas was still racked by the occasional shudder, he was not otherwise shaking, Colly thought and hoped that he was over the worst. But, mainly because she was unsure, she stayed with him. Stayed with him and held him, her love.

And gradually the shudders that had taken him began to pass. She felt him begin to relax, heard his even breathing, and she began to relax too, so much so that she closed her eyes.

She stirred in her sleep, moved—and bumped into some-one! Her eyes shot wide—she always slept alone. 'Good morning, Mrs Livingstone,' said her bed companion.

'Silas!' she exclaimed croakily, a hundred and one emotions shooting through her. 'Er—how are you?' she asked witlessly, already attempting to scuttle urgently away. Where last night, or in the early hours, she'd had her arm about his shoulders, Silas was now sitting half propped up in bed and had an arm around her shoulders, holding her there. 'I'm s-sorry,' she stammered before he could answer. 'You were shivering,' she explained hurriedly. 'I tried to keep you warm.'

'In the time-honoured way.'

'Yes—well…' She wasn't sure what he meant by that. 'I'd better go.'

'No hurry,' he replied, to her amazement. And, with a grin that she absolutely adored, 'I'm nowhere near back to my former strength yet.'

That was quite some admission, coming from him. And she checked her agitated movement to stay and look into his face for signs of the exhaustion she had witnessed there yesterday. There were none. 'Let's be thankful for small mercies,' she replied.

'For that,' Silas said, and bent over and lightly kissed her.

She adored him some more. And then made a serious attempt to move. And that was when her foot came up against a bare leg! She shot Silas a startled look: she was *under* the duvet with him! 'I didn't get into bed with you. I swear I didn't!' she protested distractedly.

'You didn't,' he agreed. 'When I woke up around six, your duvet was on the floor. You were sleeping so soundly it seemed a shame to kick you out. I covered you over.'

'You're too good to me,' she muttered, and again went to get out of bed—but his face was so near that on impulse— her brain anywhere but where it should be—she moved those extra few inches and kissed him. 'Sorry,' she mumbled. 'I'm going to have to restrain my wicked ways.' She laughed then, hoping to cover her guilt. 'Only you were so poorly, it's a relief to know you're okay and that, regardless of you ordering me not to, I did do the right thing in not calling a doctor.' She was gabbling. She broke off. 'You are all right, aren't you?'

His very dark blue eyes were looking good-humouredly down into hers. 'You tell me,' he suggested, and, his head coming down, he kissed her long and lingeringly.

'Oh!' she said on a gasp of breath when he raised his head again. Her body was all of a tingle. 'I—um—think you're stronger than you're trying to make out,' she said on a cough. Somehow the will to leave his bed has disappeared.

'I think you could be right,' he answered, and loosened the duvet so she should be free to go.

She sat up—their bodies collided. 'S-sorry,' she stammered again, made valiant efforts to leave, and got cross. 'Why am I apologising?' she exclaimed. 'You're the one who's trying to lead me astray!'

'Outrageous accusation!' he denied, and suddenly they were both laughing. Then, breaking off, they were staring at each other. And then—kissing.

And it was all too wonderful. Silas had his arms around her, she had her arms around him, his lips were seeking hers, parting her lips with his own, and his hands were holding her, warm and burning her skin. There was thunder in her ears and in her heart.

She clung to him, and kissed him as he kissed her. 'Oh,' she sighed blissfully, and quite adored him, was in another world entirely as his hands began to caress over her back. 'I'm not s-sure this is good for you,' she murmured in one isolated sane moment.

'I'll be the judge of that,' he breathed against her throat, and the next she knew she was lying half beneath him and his hand was somehow beneath her nightdress, stroking upwards.

Shock hit her—his caressing hand strayed higher. *'No!'* she cried urgently, her head in panic—but surely she'd got that wrong; she'd meant yes. She wanted him.

'No?' he queried.

'This isn't... You... Stop!' she ordered, when once more his caressing hand began to adventure.

His hand stilled. Stayed on her upper thigh—but stilled. He bent and tenderly kissed her—and she was lost. 'This could be the best medicine so far for the both of us—wouldn't you agree?' he asked against her mouth.

The words 'yes, oh, yes,' were already forming—but that was when the doorbell sounded. Colly shot a startled look to the bedside clock. Half past eight. *Half past eight!* 'Mrs Varley!' she cried, with a strangled kind of sound, and leapt out of bed, galvanised—and hurtled to her room.

Mrs Varley had her own key and would let herself in. To ring the bell was a mere courtesy because she knew there was someone there, Colly realised, as she rushed to get showered and dressed.

She was almost dressed when a whole barrage of complications hit her. Had Mrs Varley not arrived when she had then she and Silas might well have made love. On thinking about it, Colly knew there was no 'might well have' about it. She had put up all the resistance of which she was capable and, as Silas had said, he was feeling stronger than he had believed. But where would that have got them? Their marriage would have been consummated. And, while Silas still wanted that marriage certificate, what he definitely did not want was a wife.

That thought stirred her pride into action. Complications aside, she felt it incumbent on her to let him know that as he did not want a wife so she did not want a husband.

She remembered his kisses and could not lie to herself—she wanted more of them. To be in his arms... But this would never do. She recalled her response, the way she had clung to him—she had more or less offered herself to him! She recalled the way her lips had so willingly, so urgently met his—and died a hundred deaths. Oh, how was she ever to look him in the eye again?

That was when, too truly het-up to bear it, Colly decided that she did not have to look him in the eye again. She had intended to be away before his mother got here this morning anyway.

It seemed to Colly that, later than she had meant to be, she had better get her skates on. Paula Livingstone could arrive at any moment. If she hurried, Colly realised, she might be able to be away without having to see Silas again either.

Colly did not merely hurry—she flew!

CHAPTER SIX

COLLY did not see Silas again. She heard from him, though.
The next day. Flowers arrived. 'Thank you—for everything',
the card said, ending 'Silas'. How final was that?

She wanted to hate him that he could cast her off with a
few flowers, and owned she was not best pleased. Even so,
she just did not have the heart to toss his flowers in the bin.
And, since they filled two vases, she supposed that 'a few
flowers' was a bit of an understatement.

And, in all honesty, what had she expected? She had left
his apartment without a word. Had he wanted to thank her
personally, she had denied him that chance.

Day followed day just the same, she discovered, when a
month had dawdled by since that day she had walked out of
Silas's apartment. While her chief concern was to know how
his recovery was going—and, after the finality of his flowers,
to ring and ask was totally out of the question—other matters,
minor in comparison, were about.

For one, Colly had her interview for the foundation course
she'd applied for, and was accepted to start in September. For
another, Nanette sought her out at the art gallery and bluntly
stated that, since Colly was going to benefit when the sale of
the house went through, she could come and help clear everything out.

That, apart from calling in antiques valuers, Nanette had
small intention of lifting a finger was neither here nor there.
Colly was glad to be busy. It was a large house—her days
were fully occupied. Her evenings less so.

Tony Andrews continued to ask her out, and, while she had
no intention of going out with him, she started to form the

opinion that he was not so bad after all. He hadn't pushed it
when she had let him know that the evening ended on her
doorstep, had he?

And, anyway, with a month passing since she had zipped
up her overnight bag and rocketed out of Silas's apartment,
she felt that Silas had to be better by now. And a well-again
Silas, when she recalled the virile look of the man, meant that
no way was he sitting at home evenings; well, not by himself,
he wasn't.

The next time Tony Andrews phoned and suggested they
dine together somewhere, Colly agreed.

'You said yes!' he exclaimed.

Already she was half regretting her decision. 'I should love
to have dinner with you,' she said quickly, before she could
change her mind.

She knew, though, when twenty-four hours later she waited
for him to call, that her acceptance had stemmed from being
pricked by spiteful barbs of jealousy that Silas would have
renewed *his* dating activities. She had to admit, too, that the
hope of dislodging Silas from being so constantly in her heart
and her head had something to do with her decision to go out
with Tony.

Which effort was totally defeated when, on entering the
smart eating establishment Tony had chosen, the first person
she should cast her eyes on was none other than Silas
Livingstone!

The restaurant was crowded, dozens of other people were
there. So why should he stand out from the crowd? It was a
question she had no need to ask. He was her love, her life—
pure and simple.

Silas had spotted her too; she knew that he had. He was
with a party of other people; she refused to try and pinpoint
which of the attractive women in the group he was with. But
as her eyes locked on him, so for a split second his eyes seem
to lock with hers.

She turned away and looked at Tony, who was beaming his best smile down on her. Then the head waiter was leading them to their table and her fast-beating heart slowed down to a sprint. From what she could see Silas looked fully recovered from the bug that had flattened him. And she could not have been more pleased about that. She could not deny, either, that even if jealous darts were giving her a bad time she was still the same glad to have seen him.

Colly bucked her ideas up. Tony was doing his best to be an ideal dinner companion. She had agreed to dine with him, and politeness, if nothing else, said she should forget the party of six who appeared to be having a splendid time.

So she ate, while barely knowing what she ate. And she chatted and responded cheerfully to any comment Tony made. But, oh, how she heartily wished that the evening were over.

She knew that she was not going to completely relax until Silas and his party had gone. But she had struggled through to the dessert stage of her meal before she glimpsed some of the people Silas had been with making their way to the exit.

She determined to keep her eyes fixed either on her plate or Tony. She might want to look her fill at Silas, but, on the rarest chance he might cast a glance over to her, he would not find her looking at him again.

'Hello, Colly.'

So much for her decision not to look at him. She looked up, realising that Silas must have left the people he had been with to come and stand right next to her. But while her heart pounded, and before she could find her voice, he, to her astonishment, did no more than bend down and kiss her cheek in greeting!

Feeling too stunned to be able to think, let alone think straight, 'Hello,' was all she was capable of mumbling.

Silas was not a bit fazed. 'How have you been?' he asked pleasantly.

Since the last time he had seen her—when she had run from his bed? 'Er—busy,' she answered.

'Busy?' he queried, quite well aware that she now worked only one day a week.

'The house is being sold,' she replied, guessing he would know she meant her old home. 'I'm spending a lot of time there—er—clearing up.'

Plainly he was bored with such detail. She saw his glance go to her dinner companion. 'Aren't you going to introduce us?' he enquired.

It passed her by totally that he was upbraiding her for her lack of manners; she was still feeling flabbergasted that not only had he come over to their table, but he had actually kissed her.

By this time Tony was on his feet. 'Tony Andrews,' he introduced himself.

'Silas Livingstone,' Silas supplied, and the two shook hands.

She saw Tony register that Silas was *the* Silas Livingstone of Livingstone Developments, and realised that with Tony being in public relations perhaps it was part and parcel of his job to know who anybody was. But at last she found her voice, to quickly butt in, 'You're well again now, Silas?'

Both men turned to her. 'Thanks to your—personal—nursing,' Silas replied smoothly. And she wondered how she could love him so much yet at one and the same time want to punch his head. All too obviously that 'personal' was a reference to the way she had lain with him when he'd had the shivers.

'I didn't know you included nursing in your many other talents?' Tony queried, sounding curious. She wondered which hat he was wearing: his PR hat, where he soaked up any useful snippet, or if it was just idle interest.

'I should have been lost without Colly there to keep me warm,' Silas answered before she could reply.

She stared at him, stupefied. 'Silas had a fever. You may

have read about it.' She smiled at Tony while at the same time speculating if it would cause very much of a scene if right there and then she handbagged this man she was married to. 'I should think you'll consider it very carefully before you venture to the tropics again.' She smiled at Silas.

He looked her straight in the eyes. 'It had its compensations,' he murmured, nodded to Tony—and went to rejoin his party.

'I didn't know you knew Silas Livingstone?' Tony questioned the moment he was out of earshot.

'He knew my father,' she replied. 'My father was in engineering too.'

'So that's how you know him,' Tony documented. 'Um—you sound very well acquainted?'

'I was at a loose end when he was sick,' she explained, as though casually. 'I haven't seen him in ages. How's your mother?'

Tony took the hint. Then took her home. And, she was glad to note, was on his best behaviour. Though whether that was because he was remembering the last time he had brought her home, and the ages it had been before she'd agreed to go out with him again, she did not know. Or maybe he was just trying another tack. Or maybe, she mused, he had just gone off her.

Colly had proof that Tony Andrews had not gone off her when the very next evening he rang, ostensibly for a chat, but in actual fact to see how she felt about going out with him again.

While she supposed it was flattering to have someone that keen, she had barely finished thanking him for a pleasant evening the night before and thought it was too soon. No way was she looking for a steady boyfriend—though she did not doubt that she was not the only female he asked out.

'I'm busy with the house just now,' she excused, having

last night explained about her involvement with clearing her old home.

'But that's during the day,' he pointed out.

Colly had no intention of arguing. 'I'll call you, Tony,' she said decisively.

Barely had she put the phone down than it rang a second time. She suspected that it was Tony again, perhaps about to enquire just when he might expect her to ring. She just did not need this, and almost let the phone ring until he got tired. But, against that, she had dined with him last night, and he had behaved himself when he'd brought her home.

She picked up the phone. 'Hello,' she said.

'Who were you talking to?' asked a voice that set her heart-beats pounding.

'When?' she asked, striving to get herself together. Silas!

'You've been on the phone for an age!' he accused.

'Well, you know how it is when you're popular!'

'Tony Andrews?'

His question sounded like another accusation. 'Tony,' she confirmed.

Silence, then, shatteringly, 'You have remembered you're married to *me*?' Silas demanded.

Her mouth fell open. 'Get you!' she exclaimed, stunned. But, recovering fast, and feeling not a little cross at what she thought he was hinting, 'I haven't committed adultery, if that's what you're asking!' she flew. And, starting to feel angry that he'd dared to ring to say what he had—this was all too one-sided as far as she was concerned, 'I trust you can say the same?' she snapped spiritedly, knowing darn well that he could not.

But, to shatter her further, 'Believe it or not, I take my vows seriously,' Silas replied. Her mouth fell open again in shock. Marriage vows, did he mean? She realised that he did—must do. Vows encompassed marriage vows—which must mean that he had not been to bed with anyone since their marriage? Strangely enough, she believed him, and suddenly she was glad he could not see her—she would hate him to see the delighted smile that that information had wrought. She tried for something either witty or sharp to say, but found she was stunned into silence, until, 'Have dinner with me?' Silas invited.

'No!' It did not take any thinking about. Theirs was not a 'have dinner with me' relationship. He knew that too. So why was he suggesting it? 'Why?' she asked bluntly, suspiciously.

There was a pause, then—and she was sure she heard a smile in his voice— 'I might have a proposition to put to you,' he hinted.

Yes, yes, yes. He had proposed they marry. He had also proposed she go and stay at his apartment for a few nights—and look what had happened. 'I've had some of your propositions!' she retorted sharply, and, knowing that the yes, yes, yes part of her was within an ace of taking over, she promptly slammed down the phone.

No sooner was it done than Colly regretted doing so. But she went to bed smiling and knowing that she loved Silas more than ever. Which seemed to make it a good idea to keep well away from the man. But, oh, how she would dearly love to have dinner with him.

Silas did not ring again. She did not expect him to. That did not stop her heartbeats from racing, though, on the few times when the phone did ring. She wondered why he had phoned at all, and doubted that he'd had any proposition to put to her, or that he had telephoned with the sole purpose of asking her to have dinner with him. Which meant, then, that he must have rung only to remind her that she was married to him.

She would have liked to get excited at how possessive that 'You have remembered you're married to *me*?' had sounded. But in reality she knew that Silas, perhaps thinking that she and Tony were closer than they were, had only phoned to remind her that their marriage was secret and that there was an unwritten 'no immediate divorce' clause to it.

It was a lovely June morning when Colly looked out of her window at the bright sunlight—and felt that life seemed somehow to be unutterably dull. She had not seen or heard from Silas in weeks.

She reminded herself that theirs was supposed to be a noncommunications type of marriage, and tried to count her blessings. Nanette was currently away, holidaying with 'a friend', and the house was in the process of being sold; once all the legal work had been completed she'd no longer need to have any contact with her.

Tony Andrews was still asking her out. He'd obviously decided not to wait for her call and frequently phoned her. She still worked every Tuesday at the gallery—and Rupert was still bending her ear with the tragedy of his love-life.

And that was the crux of the matter. The reason why she felt so down. She did not crave a love-life; she just craved to see Silas. But he never got in touch, and he would think it mightily peculiar if, for no especial reason, she took it upon herself to contact him.

Colly gave herself a short sharp lecture on how she was going to beat this thing. She was not, not, not going to let her feelings for Silas ruin her life. Maybe when she had started that foundation course she would meet other people, get to know other people, let her life take a new direction.

But for now she was going to start a new life—with the people she knew. She rang Tony Andrews. 'Colly!' he exclaimed, sounding pleased to hear her.

Already she was regretting what she was about. But that was not the way it was supposed to go. 'I wondered if you'd like to have dinner with me?' she invited.

'Would I ever!' he accepted eagerly. 'At your apartment, do you mean?'

No, she had not meant that at all. But she hesitated—get a

life. 'If that's all right with you,' she answered. 'We can eat out if you prefer...'

'I'll bring a bottle. What time?'

He thought she meant tonight! Colly was about to put him off when her new-found self asserted itself. Why was she dithering? What better than to start her new life *now*? Tonight? This very Monday? What was there to wait for?

'We could eat about eight?' she suggested.

'I'll be there at seven-thirty,' he accepted readily.

Colly was still squashing down that part of her that was not too happy about having Tony in the apartment when, punctually at seven-thirty, bottle of wine in hand, he arrived.

It was the first time she had entertained in the apartment, and as the evening wore on so she began to lose any small feeling of apprehension; the evening seemed to be going rather well. Tony appeared impressed with her cooking—though she did confess that the stilton and celery soup was not home-made, but came from the delicatessen.

The rest of the meal was home-made, though, and it pleased her to see Tony tucking in. He seemed thoroughly relaxed, and that made her feel relaxed too. She thought she had got to know him quite well over these past months of phone calls and his visits to the gallery. But she knew she would never regard him as more than a friend.

Something she rather belatedly realised he had not taken on board when, insisting despite her protests that he wanted to help her with the dishwashing, and taking no heed of her, 'Honestly, I'd much prefer to do it later when you've gone,' he carried their dessert plates out to the kitchen and started to run the hot water.

'Let me try my hand at being domesticated,' he requested, giving her his most charming smile.

Perhaps she was too intense. To her way of thinking he was a guest, and this was his first meal in her home. Should there be subsequent meals, then perhaps to let him clear away might be in order, but...

'If you're sure.' She gave in, and took over at the sink. But only to grow immediately uptight when he passed behind her and she felt him drop a kiss on the back of her neck.

Instinctively she took a sudsy hand out from the dishwashing water to wipe his kiss away. 'Now look what you've done,' he teased, and, taking up a hand towel, he stepped closer and dabbed at her damp nape.

'That's fine. Thank you,' Colly said as lightly as she could, half turning, her instincts suddenly on the alert as she took a step back from him. She at once came up against the kitchen sink—Tony moved in closer.

He took the towel and dried her hands. 'You're beautiful— you know that, don't you?' he said, to her amazement his tone suddenly gone all seductive. She was still staring at him mesmerised when he reached out and took her in his arms.

'This—isn't getting the washing up done,' she reminded him, staying the polite hostess.

'We can, as you suggested, do it later,' he replied, and kissed her.

Colly felt a soul in torment. She wanted a life, had to have a life without Silas. But the wretched truth was there undeniably before her—she did not want anyone's kisses but his.

'You can do better than that, can't you?' Tony coaxed— and she wondered if she was being fair to him, fair to herself?

'Of course,' she replied, and tried. She put her arms around him and offered him her lips. But he was alien to hold, his lips alien. It will get better, she attempted to tell herself, in despair about the new life she was going to make for herself if only she could put some kind of effort into it.

He came closer, pressing her against the sink. She tried hard to keep calm, to respond; did she really want to do this? She was wedged in between him and the sink with no way out when he placed his hands on her hips and pulled her into him.

She pushed him away and knew then that, new life or no new life, she would much rather do the washing up. 'Er—I think...' was as far as she got before Tony grabbed her and clamped his moist mouth over hers, his body pressing into her while his hands moved up, seeking her breasts. *'No!'* she yelled, and, giving him a push, meant it.

He knew she meant it too. It was there in her tone, her look, her stance. 'Why not?' he argued. 'Hell's bells, I've given you miles of rope to get you to this pitch. You invite me to dinner and then...' He grinned suddenly—she saw it as a leer—'You still playing hard to get, Colly?' he questioned, and made another grab for her.

She was determined not to panic, but knew she was losing it when, forcefully, she ordered, *'No!'*

'Oh, come on.' He made another lunge for her.

'No!' she said again.

'Why not?' he repeated, a wheedling kind of note there in his voice. 'What's to stop us? I'm unattached. You're free and...' he leered again '...I'm sure I could make you willing. Relax, sweetie,' he pressed, his breath hot against her face, and in the next moment he had fastened his lips on hers again.

Her agitation was growing as again she pushed him wildly away, while wondering at the same time how, when she now felt revolted by his kisses, she had allowed him to kiss her in the first place. And suddenly, her composure shot when he would not take his wet mouth from hers, she gave him another shove, and, picking up on what he had just said, cried, 'I'm not free!'

That seemed to stop him in his tracks. He stared incredulously at her. 'You're—engaged—married?' he asked in disbelief.

Oh, Lord, her head was spinning. She did not know where the devil she was. All she could think then was that no one must know about her marriage. Panic set in with a vengeance. 'We're getting divorced!' It was out before she could stop it.

Tony heard what she had said, for all she had gabbled it out in a panicky rush, and sifted through what she had just told him. 'So where's the problem?' he came back, without so much as a blink. But even as he went to make a grab for her again, so part of his brain appeared to be putting two and two together. 'Where's your husband?' he asked, and, more pertinently, 'Who *is* your husband?' he prodded further. And, his two and two swiftly adding up to a correct four, before she could halt him, 'Silas Livingstone!' he exclaimed, sounding staggered, though still able to replay in his mind that time when Silas Livingstone had revealed that she had 'personally' nursed him when he had been ill. How she had been there to keep him warm. 'You're married to Silas Livingstone!' he concluded, and, as if shaken anew, he actually took a step back.

Colly wanted to repeat that they were getting divorced— but suddenly a whole welter of complications were crashing in. She immediately wanted to deny that she and Silas were married at all. And from there at once grew terrified that any other panic-stricken comment she might make would see her saying something else to Tony that could lead just about anywhere.

Without another word she went smartly from the kitchen. Tony followed. 'It's true, isn't it?' he questioned, but seemed to know it for a fact.

'I—think you'd better go, Tony,' she replied, trying to keep her voice from shaking.

'That's a bit steep, isn't it?' he complained. 'You invite me for an intimate dinner...'

Intimate dinner! Was that the way he had read her invitation? She shook her head. 'I've enjoyed your company,' she told him—which, up to a point, she had. 'But I never intended it to be more than dinner.'

'I don't suppose your husband would approve,' Tony, his tone changing, offered sourly. There wasn't any possible an-

swer to that. So she just stood her ground. After a few belligerent moments, 'Don't call me—I'll call you,' he said huff-
ily. Colly went and opened the door for him. Seriously
annoyed, he took the none-too-subtle hint.

She closed the door after him, reeling. What had she done?
Just what…? It all played back horribly in her head. 'Silas
Livingstone!' he had guessed. 'We're getting divorced,' she
had lied. Oh, save us!

In need of something to do, Colly went to the kitchen and
carried on with the dishes from where she had left off. But
her head was spinning even more when the used dishes had
been washed, dried and put away, and the kitchen once more
immaculate. Because by then she had recalled that Tony
Andrews worked in public relations, and, from conversations
she'd had with him, she had also recalled that he seemed well
acquainted with people in the news media.

Oh, heavens. What was to stop him making capital in any
way he could from what she had so unintentionally revealed?
She doubted that after tonight's little episode Tony would feel
any loyalty to her.

Needing action of any kind, she went and brushed her teeth.
Then ran a comb through her hair. But she was so unable to
settle she began to pace up and down. For herself she could
not care less what Tony told his press contacts. For Silas…
She could not think. The whole thing was a nightmare.

She continued to pace up and down, but as the hands on
her watch neared half past eleven it came to her that there
was only one thing she could possibly do. She had to warn
Silas! There was no way around it; she had to warn him.

Hoping that he was in—and for all his statement that he
took his vows seriously it would not stop him from living it
up somewhere—Colly went and found his home number.

When the phone was not answered straight away she was
sure he must be out. But then, doing nothing for the agitat-

ed mass she was inside, the phone was picked up and, 'Livingstone,' he answered.

'It—it's Colly,' she stammered.

Silence for a moment, before, 'You make a habit of telephoning men when they've gone to bed for the night?' he questioned tersely.

And she was glad he was being vile. It made some—not all, but some—of her nerves subside. 'I have it on good authority that you're in bed alone!' she retorted snappily. But was immediately unsure, sick inside with jealousy, and nervous again. 'You are, aren't you? I m-mean, I haven't…?' She could not finish.

An agonising moment or two of silence followed, until, 'You haven't,' Silas confirmed, and his tone thawing a little, 'To be quite honest, petal, I have to get to the airport for a business trip very soon—I wouldn't mind a few hours' sleep before then.'

'Oh, I'm sorry—I'm sorry,' she apologised. But, as the import of what he had just said hit her, 'You're going away!' she cried.

'Don't upset yourself—I'm coming back.'

Smug pig. 'This isn't funny!' she exclaimed furiously.

'Presumably you're going to get to the point of this call—before my plane takes off.'

'You weren't smacked enough as a child!' she flew, feeling very much like redressing the balance had he been near.

His tone changed again, was warmer again. 'You're in a tizz about something?' he guessed.

Colly promptly folded. 'Oh, Silas,' she mourned. 'I've done something so dreadful I hardly know how to tell you.'

'Sounds—serious,' he commented.

'It is. It—um—won't wait until you get back.'

Silas was decisive. 'I'd better come over.'

'No, no,' she protested. 'I've enough guilt without adding

any more. You get what sleep you can. I'll come to you.' She put the phone down before he should persuade her differently.

A short while later she was ringing the doorbell to his apartment, and still had not been able to find a way of telling him what she knew she urgently had to share with him.

He was wearing shirt and trousers when he opened the door. 'You needn't have dressed,' came tripping off her tongue, she having assumed that, having got up from his bed, he would be robe-clad.

'Now, there's an invitation,' he said dryly, leading the way to the drawing room.

She gave him a speaking look, but as he indicated she take a seat and then took a seat facing her, so Colly saw the opening that she needed. 'That's the thing about invitations,' she began, searching for words and finding a few, 'I invited a friend to dinner tonight—and got things very badly wrong.'

'Tony Andrews?' Silas guessed, a hard kind of glint all at once there in his eyes.

'I do know other men,' she stated, a touch miffed that he seemed to think Tony was the only man who asked her out. But she was in the wrong here and she knew it; this was not the time to get shirty. 'But, yes, Tony.'

'Where did you eat?' Silas wanted to know.

She suspected he already knew. 'At the apartment,' she owned.

'My grandfather's apartment?' he asked toughly.

'It's where I live!' she snapped.

'Andrews often dines there with you?'

There was no let-up on Silas's toughness, she noted. But after what she had done she wasn't in a position to take exception to anything. 'It was the first—and the last—time,' she confessed.

Silas had an alert look in his eyes, but his tough tone was fading as he commented, 'It sounds as if you sent him home with a flea in his ear?'

'I—it…not quite. But—' on reflection '—similar.' Then suddenly she wanted this all said and done. If Silas was going to rain coals of fury down on her head, and she was sure he would go ballistic, then the sooner it was done the better. 'Well, the thing is, I—er—invited him to dinner out of friendship. But he—um—seemed to think I'd invited him for an—er—intimate dinner, and…'

'It didn't occur to you that dinner for two at your place might be construed as a touch intimate?'

'Well, if you're going to take his side!' she erupted heatedly. But again remembered that she was the one in the wrong here. 'No,' she changed tack to answer, 'it didn't cross my mind that—that I was on the menu with the *petit fours*.'

'He came on strong and you didn't like it?' Silas guessed, his expression stern.

Colly flicked her glance from him. She did not want to tell Silas how she had tried to respond to Tony. But in all honesty she could not make Tony out to be the villain of the piece. 'It—er—was all right at first,' she admitted, but hurried on, 'Then I said no, and…'

'You said no?' Silas questioned. Her ears felt scarlet. 'Because you didn't want to? Or because you're married to me?' he persisted.

By no chance was she going to let Silas know that other men stood no chance—because of him. But she could feel herself getting het-up again at the thought that Silas might guess at her feelings for him.

Unable to sit still, but with no idea of where she was going, she was on her feet. 'Would you like me to make you some coffee?' she offered.

'Because you didn't want to or because of your marriage vows?' Silas insisted.

She felt cornered. 'Because I just don't sleep around!' she said heatedly, and saw that Silas looked somewhat shaken by her confession.

'You don't?' he queried, on his feet too. 'Hmm—you have, though?' She would not answer, but then found he was persistent if nothing else. 'At some time you have—experimented—fully?'

She still did not want to answer. Silence reigned until, dumbly, she shook her head, finding the carpet of great interest. 'How old-fashioned is that?' she asked, and, expecting some derisive remark that at twenty-three she still hadn't left the starting blocks, she turned her back on him.

But to her surprise Silas made no derisive remark, but came over to her and, taking hold of her upper arms, turned her to face him. Gently then he drew her against him. 'Don't be embarrassed,' he instructed softly.

'I feel stupid,' she confessed, and for long wonderful seconds was held in his gentle hold.

Then, unhurriedly, he lowered his head and gently kissed her. 'You're not stupid, you're lovely,' he assured her, and led her back to her chair. 'So what happened when you rejected Andrews' advances?' he asked.

Feeling a little bemused—Silas's light kiss just now had had far more effect than the assault of Tony Andrews' kisses—she endeavoured to think straight. 'Well, he wouldn't take no for an answer—' she began, but was stopped from saying more when, on the instant enraged, Silas cut her off.

'He assaulted you? He sexually assaulted you?' he roared. 'Where does he live?' he demanded, on his feet and seeming about to charge off to Tony Andrews' address and flatten him.

'No. No,' Colly said quickly, realising that Silas's protection of her stemmed only from the fact that he had given her the right to use his name. It was the reaction of any decent man, but there was nothing more personal in it than that. Though she did so hope that Silas liked her. 'I think I told him no a couple of times, and he wanted to know why not— he thought I was playing hard to get,' she rushed on. 'I should never have invited him to the apartment, I can see that now.

Anyway, he couldn't see why I wouldn't. Oh, heavens, this all sounds so sordid.'

'You're doing fine,' Silas encouraged, his fury in check. 'You're getting there,' he added, as though recalling how over the phone she had said that *she* had done something so dreadful. And, as though to encourage her further, he retook his seat and stayed quiet until she was ready to go on.

'Well, Tony was—well, you know—and wanting to know what was to stop us. He said that he was unattached, and that I was free, and... Well, anyhow, I was starting to feel a touch out of my depth, so I must have grabbed at that ''out'', and I told him I wasn't free.'

'You told him you were married?'

'Not in so many words, I don't think. But then I got all over the place in my head, and all I knew was that no one must know about our marriage.'

'You weren't making a very good job of it,' Silas butted in.

'It gets worse.'

'I'll brace myself.'

'By then I was panicking.'

'Poor love,' he said, as she at one time, she clearly recalled, had said to him.

She felt a little heartened. Sufficiently, anyway, to be able to carry on. 'I knew at once that I'd said the wrong thing. Instinctively knew, I suppose, that I had to say something to counteract that I'd just as good as said I was married. She swallowed. 'I then went and dug myself into an even bigger hole.'

'You told him you were married to me?' Silas guessed.

She shook her head. 'I didn't have to. Tony guessed. He must have remembered that night you two met. You know, that night when...'

'When I commented on the fact that you'd had a hand in nursing me?'

'Such as it was—my nursing, I mean,' she said, thinking how all she had done was dole out his medication. But as she recalled waking up in bed with him, so she blushed scarlet. 'A-anyhow...' she tried to rush on.

'Anyhow, from that Andrews deduced that the man you were married to must be me,' Silas took up, with a not unkind look at her blushing face. 'Is that it?' he wanted to know.

'I said it gets worse,' Colly reminded him quietly. And, wanting it all said and done, she hurriedly added. 'Tony works in PR. He knows all sorts of press people—' She broke off when she spotted the sharp look that came to Silas's eyes.

'You foresee a problem?' He was ahead of her; she knew that he was.

This was it. She had to tell him. She took a deep breath, but had she been hoping it might steady her, she knew it had failed. She was shaking inside as she blurted out, 'I was panicking, and I knew I had to do something to counteract that I'd as good as told him that I was married. I just wasn't thinking,' she confessed, 'and I told him that we were—um—getting divorced.'

Silas stared at her as if he could not believe his hearing. 'You told him that you and I were going to divorce?' he questioned harshly. 'You actually told this man with press connections that you and I were divorcing? When you know, have always known, that that is the last piece of information I want broadcast—'

'I'm sorry,' she cut in miserably, watching as Silas, as if needing to be on his feet, left his chair. 'I was in panic, as I said—trying to make good something I'd inadvertently let slip—that I wasn't free.'

Silas seemed gone from her, his look thoughtful. She would dearly love to know what was going on behind his clever forehead. 'What chance is there that Andrews won't make capital out of this?' he wanted to know.

'I've no idea. He was pretty mad at me when he left, so I

don't suppose he's likely to want to spare me. Shall I ring him?' she asked. 'Appeal to him not to—'

'No!' Silas answered decisively. And, his thoughts and conclusions soon reached, he resumed his seat, and looked her straight in the eye as he informed her, 'I want you to have nothing whatsoever to do with Andrews in the future.' And, his chin jutting slightly, 'Is that understood?' he stressed.

'I'm not so keen myself,' she agreed, and was rewarded with a near smile. 'Is there anything I can do?' she asked, hoping Silas would not say that in his view she had done more than enough.

He did not say anything of the sort. But nor did his smile make it when he let her into his deliberations. 'All things considered, there is only one thing we *can* do if I'm to be able to continue to make long-term plans for Livingstone Developments.' Her eyes were fixed on nowhere but him when, coolly, he brought out, 'Thanks to you, my dear, I believe the time has come to reveal that we—you and I—are married—happily married.'

Her mouth went dry. She had no idea what any of that might mean, yet knew that figuratively she hadn't a leg to stand on. She had known the rules when she had married Silas—she had known in advance that divorce was a forbidden word. She it was who had broken the rules, and it was she who had messed the whole of it up.

'Y-you intend to tell your grandfather?' she asked hesitantly.

'My father,' Silas corrected. 'He's an early riser. I'll phone him from the airport and ring my grandfather when I get back. By then he'll know from my father that you and I are married, and that despite what they might read in the press neither of us has any intention of being divorced.' And, having told her how it was to be, he stood up. She guessed he was keen to get to bed and get what sleep he could before he went to catch his early flight. Colly stood up too, and Silas escorted her to the door. 'Agreed?' he thought to ask.

Colly stared unhappily up into his searching dark blue eyes. She had no idea what sort of complications this turn of events might bring. But she had brought this sorry state of affairs about, so how could she not agree?

'Agreed,' she answered, and again wanted to apologise for whatever chain of events she had set in motion by her agitated 'I'm not free' to Tony Andrews. She did not apologise, but felt so down just then that she would dearly have loved it had Silas held her for a moment or two in a gentle hug.

But Silas did not give her a hug. Nor did he attempt to kiss her cheek. She supposed he must be as fed up with her as she was with herself.

'I'll be in touch when I get back,' he told her.

'Whatever you say,' she replied, and left.

CHAPTER SEVEN

COLLY spent the next two days searching the various newspapers for any reference to the fact that she and Silas Livingstone were married—there was none.

But, oh, what had she done? By now Silas's father, and his mother too, of course, would know that their son was married. And, by the look of it, Colly realised, she had panicked unnecessarily. With nothing in the papers there had been no need for any of his family to know that he had a wife! By now Silas's grandfather probably knew as well—but there had been absolutely no need for anyone to know! And Silas would hate her.

In an agony of torment from not knowing what, if anything, was going on, Colly felt very inclined to ring Tony Andrews and ask him if he intended to use that snippet that Silas Livingstone was married. Against ringing Tony, though, was her fear that if he had not already been in touch with his press pals, any call she made might prompt him to do so. And anyhow, Silas had been adamant that she should have nothing more to do with Tony; she supposed Silas knew more about these things than she did.

She left her bed on Thursday, wishing she had some idea of when Silas would be coming home. Oh, what a hornets' nest she had stirred up! And yet she'd had to warn him, hadn't she? And it had been his decision to, as it were, go public. And in all fairness, looking back to last Monday, when she had gone to see him, Colly still did not see how she could not have told him what she had.

To add to her inner turmoil there was nothing in the papers that day either. She had no idea if Silas would call or phone.

'I'll be in touch when I get back,' he'd said. She wished now that she had thought to ask when that would be. As it was, not wanting to miss his call, she had spent most of her time since yesterday more or less glued to the apartment.

He did not phone that day either, but it was around nine o'clock that evening when someone knocked on her door. Silas! It could be one of her neighbours, of course. She was acquainted with several of them by now, but as her heartbeats raced she somehow knew that it would be Silas.

Which caused her to take a very deep breath before she opened the door. It was him! They stared at each other. Colly sought to find her voice, but the 'Hello' she found came out sounding all husky and, to her ears, weird. 'Come in,' she invited, and left him to follow her into the sitting room. She turned. He was business-suited. 'You've come from the airport?' she enquired politely.

'I got in this afternoon. I thought I'd better spend some time in the office.'

'Have you eaten?'

If he could tell she was nervous he did not refer to it. 'I have, but I wouldn't mind taking you up on your offer to make me a coffee,' he replied pleasantly.

Colly was relieved to escape to the kitchen. They had been at his apartment when she had volunteered to make him coffee. Her relief was short-lived, though, because a few seconds later Silas joined her in the kitchen.

'Andrews been in touch?' he asked conversationally.

She shook her head. 'I don't think I'm flavour of the month there,' she responded.

'Does that upset you?'

'You know better than that!' she replied shortly. But then folded completely and blurted out, 'Oh, Silas, I got it all wrong, didn't I?'

'You did?' he asked, seeming not to know what she was talking about.

'You won't know, being out of the country and everything, but there's been nothing in the papers about—about us—being married!'

'I know,' he surprised her by saying. So she could only suppose he had read the foreign editions while abroad. Either that or he had found time to scan them since his plane had landed that afternoon.

She sighed heavily. 'I'm sorry. I rather jumped the gun, didn't I—coming to see you like that? But,' she excused, 'I felt you had to know.'

'You did the only thing possible,' he assured her.

'I did?'

He smiled then, and it so lit his face that her heart turned over. How dear he was to her. 'There hasn't been anything in the press yet, but there will be tomorrow,' he said succinctly. 'Shall I carry that in?' he suggested, taking up the tray of coffee.

They were back in the sitting room—she seated on the sofa, Silas having taken the chair opposite, with the highly polished table in between. He relaxed back, seemingly enjoying the coffee he had apparently been parched for. She ignored her own coffee; there were things here that she felt she ought to know.

'You—um—seem pretty certain the—papers will be printing—'

'Just the financial ones, I suspect,' Silas chipped in, and went on to dumbfound her as he explained, 'I got in touch with my PA first thing on Tuesday. I suspected that before our marriage—or divorce—was made news, someone would contact my office for verification. At the end of my instructions Ellen knew to confirm, if pushed, that I was happily married, to laugh at any suggestion that a divorce might be in the offing, and to then transfer the call to my own PR department, who would quote that which I had dictated to Ellen.'

Colly stared at him. 'Forward planning has nothing on you,' she said faintly. And, endeavouring to recover, 'And someone did ring?'

'Several people,' he confirmed.

'Am I allowed to know what this piece of dictation was?'

He shrugged. 'I kept any details about us to a minimum by saying that Columbine Gillingham and I had married quietly on account of your father's recent demise. And from there I took the limelight off you and me by giving details of your father's brilliant engineering brain and mentioning some of his more spectacular achievements.' Silas paused. 'I hope that doesn't offend you, Colly?'

How could it? It was true that they had married quietly, shortly after her father's death, even if his recent death was not the reason for their quiet wedding. Nor could she be offended that Silas had referred to her father's brilliant engineering brain; it heartened her that her father's engineering achievements were not forgotten.

'No,' she said simply, 'I'm not offended.' And, realising then that with the press having contacted Silas's office she had done the right thing after all in contacting him, she reached for her coffee and took a sip. A trace nervously, she had to admit, she moved on to enquire, as calmly as she could, 'You—rang your father from the airport? You—um—said you would.'

'I rang him.' He nodded, and his lips twitched a little. 'My mother was ringing my hotel in Italy before I got there.'

Oh, crumbs. 'They—your parents—they're all right about it?'

'You mean their not being present at our wedding?'

She had not meant that, though supposed they had a right to feel a touch annoyed. 'I mean more about you being married.'

'They couldn't be more pleased. Not to put too fine a point on it, my mother is overjoyed.'

'She is?'

'She is,' he confirmed. 'She remembers speaking to you on the phone—and says you have a lovely voice.' Colly stared at him. 'My father,' he went on, 'is just pleased that I'm happy.'

'You—are happy?' Colly queried.

'Why wouldn't I be?'

Why indeed? The future of Livingstone Developments appeared secure, and the future of the company was what he cared about. 'Have your parents told your grandfather yet, do you think?'

Silas looked at her solemnly, and she felt he hesitated a fraction before he confirmed that his grandfather did indeed know that he had taken himself a bride. 'My grandfather is delighted,' he revealed.

But Colly had a strange feeling that there was more than that. 'And?' she pressed, a touch apprehensively, she had to admit.

'And,' Silas replied calmly, 'my grandfather wants to meet you.'

'No!' She did not even have to think about it. 'No,' she said again, though less forcefully this time. Silas said nothing, but just sat watching her. And then Colly did start to think about it, even if she did not like the idea any better. 'When?' she asked.

'He'd like us to visit this weekend.'

This weekend! *Weekend?* 'Weekend?' she questioned faintly. 'You mean a *whole* weekend?' Well, that wasn't on. Whatever excuses Silas had to make, he could jolly well get them out of it.

'He's very lonely since my grandmother died.' Silas, whether he knew it or not, jangled her heartstrings. 'But, in view of our other commitments, I said we'd arrive on Saturday—rather than the Friday he suggested—and stay just the one night.'

Stay one night: Colly did not feel any happier, but something else Silas had just said caused her to forget that for the moment and follow this new trail. 'Our—other commitments?' she queried warily—and was right to be wary, she very soon discovered.

'Quite naturally my parents will be most offended if they don't get to meet you first,' Silas explained.

Colly did not think very much of his explanation! She owned that her brain did not seem to be working at full capacity just then, but it very much appeared that if she was to meet Silas's grandfather on Saturday—and bearing in mind that today, or tonight, was Thursday—then at some time between now and then she must first meet Silas's parents.

'This is getting much too complicated,' she complained, casting a belligerent look over to the man she had 'quietly' married.

He bore her look pleasantly. 'What's complicated?' he asked, and sounded so reasonable she could have truly done with hating him.

Particularly since she could not come up with much of an answer. 'Why can't we just tell your parents the truth? That we are married, but—'

'Because to do so would put them under an obligation not to tell my grandfather the truth,' Silas cut in heavily. 'This is my situation, not theirs.'

Reluctantly Colly could see that. To involve his parents in the way she had suggested would just not be fair to them. But she protested just the same. 'I don't like deceiving people,' she said woodenly.

'How are we deceiving anyone?' he asked, and she truly did hate him that while she was starting to feel all stewed up he could continue to sound so reasonable. She gave him a look of dislike. It bounced off him. And he was still insufferably reasonable when he drew her attention to the facts.

'My grandfather wants to meet my wife—you, Colly, *are* my wife.'

You are my wife. She found it hard to hate him while her heart took a giddy trip at those words. But, though those lovely words sounded beautifully possessive, she knew full well that Silas stated them as merely fact. Colly pulled herself sternly together. 'I didn't sign up for any of this when I agreed to marry you,' she reminded him snappily.

'Neither did I!' he returned bluntly. And, his expression harsh, 'As I recall, it was you who let the cat out,' he reminded her.

He had her there. If she had not let Tony Andrews know she was not free, and then gone on to compound that error by telling him she was getting divorced—giving him space to speculate on whom she might be married to—none of this would be happening. As it was, Silas had been forced into taking what action he had to when she'd triggered off that which could have led to disaster.

She was in the wrong, and she knew it. Colly took a defeated breath and, as graciously as she could in the circumstances, enquired, 'When do I meet your parents?'

His harsh expression faded. 'We're having them over for dinner tomorrow evening.'

'Over at your place?' she asked, her voice barely audible— keep reminding yourself that you're the one in the wrong, Colly.

'Over at *our* place,' he corrected.

'You're not expecting me to move in with you?' she asked in sudden alarm.

He looked cheered. 'Oh, your face!' he exclaimed, but sobered to let her know, 'As far as anyone else knows we live together, but at this stage I see no need for us to go that far.'

Why did she feel miffed at what he said? She did not want to live with him, for goodness' sake—well, not under the present circumstances, she qualified.

'We must be thankful for small mercies, I suppose,' she offered dryly, and saw his lips twitch, felt a moment's weakness where he was concerned, but hurried on, 'I'm cooking?'

'Mrs Varley will attend to that. My parents will be at my place around seven, but just in case they should be half an hour early, if you could be there around six?'

'You'll be there—at six?'

'I'll finish work early,' he said, and suddenly Colly was feeling dreadful.

'I've caused one almighty giant upheaval, haven't I?' she said apologetically.

'Oh, Colly, don't be too upset,' Silas said gently, leaving his chair and coming over to take a seat on the sofa with her. And, his tone friendly, not sharp, as she felt she deserved, 'One way and another you have done me a favour.'

She turned in her seat to look at him, her heart pounding to have him so close. 'How?' she asked with what sign of normality she could find. 'If I hadn't—'

'I find it next to impossible to tell lies to my family,' Silas cut in. 'So when my father asked me outright if I'd thought any more about what he'd confided about grandfather altering his will I was able to calm his anxieties and truthfully tell him I was seriously involved with someone.'

'You meant me?'

'You,' Silas confirmed. 'By then you and I were married.'

'I don't suppose you can truthfully get more seriously involved than that,' she mumbled.

'Everything slotted in for both my father and my mother when they recalled how, when I was in hospital, you were allowed in to see me. How, when I got out of hospital, you were at my apartment staying with me. My mother really started to get her hopes high then, by the way. When, less than a couple of months after that, said cat bolted out from the bag, it didn't seem so far-fetched to them when I explained that we had quietly married.'

'They didn't think it at all odd that we didn't invite them to our wedding?'

'Not so much when I told them your maiden name—who you were. My father at once recognised your name. He had been with me, paying his respects at your father's funeral. My mother, while a triftle put out, it has to be said, at the same time understood when I said I didn't want to wait but wanted to marry straight away. That, with your father's death so recent, we'd agreed we did not want a big tell-the-world type of wedding.'

Colly knew, for all her heart had given a little flutter, that she could not get excited about that 'I didn't want to wait'. Silas had wanted that marriage certificate with all speed—she, his bride, was incidental to his forward planning.

'Um...' she murmured, and saw she had his full attention. 'Er—this dinner tomorrow...' she began, hardly knowing how to continue. Silas looked at her, but was not saying another word, and she felt forced to continue, 'I mean, do your parents think ours is a love-match?' There—it was out.

'I haven't said so in as many words. But my mother certainly will be sure that ours is a love-match. Or—' suddenly he was grinning a wicked grin '—or at least that no woman could know me and not love me.'

'Which just goes to show how terribly blinkered mothers really are!' Colly said acidly. And because it was so true that she did love him, so very much—only he was not to know it—she got up from the sofa commenting, 'I just thought I ought to know—er—whether I'm supposed to—um—show a bit of affection for you.'

'Well, if your feelings really do get too much for you, and you feel you just have to hold and kiss me...' he began to tease. Then, seeing how tense she suddenly seemed, he left the sofa and came to stand next to her. 'Nervous about tomorrow?' he asked kindly.

Petrified, if you must know. 'You could say that,' she replied, and suddenly found herself in the loose hold of his embrace.

'Don't be,' he said softly, as her heart went into overdrive. 'My parents will love you. Just be yourself and everything will be fine.'

She wished she could believe him. The truth was, she did not feel she knew what was herself any more. She shook her head in some kind of bewilderment. 'All I did on Monday night was say I wasn't free, add that I was getting divorced—and now look where we are!'

'Things have moved on at something of a pace,' Silas agreed quietly.

'Something of a pace! They've positively galloped!'

'Don't fret about it. What's done is done.'

And she was the one who had done it. 'I'm throwing you out,' she told him, knowing she quite desperately needed to get herself more of one piece. Just being held in the loose circle of his arms was making her head chaotic.

'I thought you might be,' he replied, lightly kissed her cheek, and then walked to the door.

Colly did not sleep well that night. In her head she imagined all sorts of disasters at Friday night's dinner—when she would meet her in-laws. The only way she was able to get any rest at all was by repeatedly reminding herself that Silas would be there too. She would have his support.

But it was while she was showering on Friday morning that the trepidation of her thoughts about that evening let up to let in an even bigger cause for worry. And it had nothing to do with that evening—but the following one.

Because only then did something she had been too preoccupied to think about suddenly jump up and hit her. What about tomorrow evening? Or, more specifically, tomorrow night? Only then did it dawn on her that, unless Silas Livingstone Senior lived in a house that had a separate suite for overnight guests, tomorrow night she was going to have to share a room with Silas!

There was one thing about this new source of inner conflict, she discovered, it certainly transferred some of her agitation away from that evening's dinner party. She hoped with all she had that Silas had plans to sleep elsewhere. But, bearing in mind they'd barely been married four months, she could imagine his grandfather looking askance at the mere idea of them sleeping in separate rooms.

She was glad when later that morning her phone rang, and a difficult conversation with Henry Warren gave her head some respite from her concerns about meeting her in-laws—both in London and in Dorset.

'Is it true?' Henry Warren asked.

She knew what he was talking about and realised she should have guessed he would take a financial newspaper and might pick up that which Silas had dictated.

'Yes, it's true,' she replied. 'I'm sorry, Uncle Henry, I should have told you. But...' But what? He had been untold good to her, and must think her silence about something as important as this very strange. 'I've been a bit—um—mixed up,' she added lamely.

'Because of your father?'

'I—er—Silas was at my father's funeral.'

'You met him that day?'

Sort of. 'I'm sorry I didn't tell you.' She felt she had to apologise again. 'But Silas and I, we wanted a quiet wedding. His parents didn't even know about us until quite recently.'

That seemed to mollify him a little. But, maybe out of duty to his old friend, he still had questions to ask. 'But what are you doing living in that apartment alone?'

'The apartment belongs to Silas's grandfather, but he doesn't use it and doesn't wish to sell it so we sort of keep the place aired. Silas goes abroad on business from time to time, but for the moment when he's home he likes to sometimes stay here.' Colly was not at all happy about embroidering the truth the way she was doing. 'And,' she hurried on, forestalling what she anticipated would be his next question, of why she had been so relieved when he had got some funds through for her, 'Silas is more than generous,' she explained—she still had ten thousand pounds of his that he was refusing to take back— 'But I felt such a pauper going to him penniless; it was a pride thing, I suppose. I was so grateful to you when you were able to get me some money of my own.'

'You always were a proud little thing,' he commented when she had finished, and while she was swishing around in guilt he went on more warmly—perhaps he more than most was aware of the joylessness of her existence prior to her father's death. 'You deserve some happiness, Colly.'

She thanked him and, while regretting she could not be entirely open with him, felt better that their phone conversation had ended in a friendly and affectionate way.

By four that afternoon, however, thoughts of the impending evening had taken most other thoughts from her mind. She supposed it was usual for most women to be apprehensive on meeting their in-laws for the first time. Though everything, she felt, about this meeting was *un*usual.

Because of her fidgety unable-to-settle feelings, Colly left the apartment ten minutes before she should. She hoped to feel better once everything was under way. She was wearing an emerald-green chiffon-over-silk evening trouser suit and, having noticed an absence of flowers in Silas's home, was carrying a sizeable bouquet of flowers when she rang his doorbell.

She wondered who would answer the door—Silas or Mrs Varley. It was Silas. He had said he would leave work early, and had. But while she thought he looked absolutely wonderful, he seemed impressed that she had made a bit of an effort herself.

'You look just a touch gorgeous,' he said softly, not moving back to let her in, but just standing there, his eyes showing his admiration.

Theirs was a non-personal relationship—most of the time. But to hear that Silas thought she looked a touch gorgeous was what she needed to hear. 'Just something I threw on,' she murmured offhandedly, every bit as though she had not changed three times before deciding to stick with the first outfit she had tried on. And, feeling unutterably shy suddenly, she thrust the flowers at him, 'Here,' she said, 'take a hold of these before they die.'

His face was alight with laughter as he took the hint and invited her in. She felt good suddenly. Perhaps the evening would not be such a trial after all.

'Where do you keep your vases?' Colly asked as they went along the hall.

'Good question.'

She wanted to grin—it was good just to be with him. 'I'll try the kitchen,' she decided, and found he was right there with her when she went in that direction.

In the kitchen was where Mrs Varley was, putting the finishing touches to a smoked salmon and watercress starter. 'Oh, Mrs Livingstone.' Mrs Varley beamed before Colly could say a word, and Colly hid her small moment of shock—but owned she was delighted at being so addressed. 'Mr Livingstone has told me of your marriage.' And, clearly a born romantic, 'I know you're both going to be very happy.' She beamed again.

'Thank you,' Colly answered. She felt stumped to know what to say next, but beamed a smile back and asked, 'Am I going to be in your way if I arrange the flowers in here?'

It took longer for her to arrange the flowers than she had thought—they just did not go right—and Colly was glad she had arrived ten minutes early. But by a quarter to seven there were two flower arrangements brightening up the otherwise masculine-looking drawing room, and one arrangement in the dining room.

Her chores, if chores they were, completed, Colly was starting to feel more nervous than ever. Mrs Varley assured her she had everything under control, so Colly left her and went to the bathroom to check her appearance. She ran a comb through her hair, touched up her lipstick and left the bathroom. Wishing the evening were over, she went to the drawing room. Silas was there waiting for her.

Whether or not he could tell she was being attacked by nerves she had no idea, but he smiled a smile that warmed her heart, and, coming over to her, asked, 'What would you like to drink?'

How he could sound so unconcerned when she felt such a wreck, she had no idea. But she drew strength from his easy manner. 'Nothing, thanks,' she refused. She had warned him that she was no good at subterfuge, but if he still wanted this evening to go ahead, so be it.

He took her refusal to have a drink without comment, but continued to come towards her, halting barely a step away. 'Perhaps you'd better wear this,' he said, and, putting his hand into his pocket, took out the wedding ring she had returned to him.

'I forgot!' she exclaimed, realising that while some women might prefer not to wear a wedding ring, she was not one of them. And, as he had once before, Silas took a hold of her left hand and slipped the gold band over her marriage finger.

'You're shaking!' he remarked in surprise at her trembling hand.

She felt absurd. He was so sophisticated, so able to carry off any situation. 'It's all right for you!' she accused snappily. 'You know my in-laws. I don't!'

He burst out laughing. 'Oh, I do l—like you, Colly Livingstone,' he said, and while her heart raced at the sudden warm look in his eyes, so the doorbell sounded.

'They're early!' she gasped.

'It's the season,' he said, and to her gratitude did not leave her alone to wait while he went to let his parents in, but caught hold of her hand. 'Come on—let's go and get it done,' he said, and led her to the door.

The next few minutes passed in a haze of beaming smiles of hugs and kisses that left Colly, who had missed a mother's love, feeling very emotional.

'How beautiful you are!' Paula Livingstone exclaimed, tall, distinguished and all heart. 'And, oh, how pleased I am to meet you.' She was still bursting with joy when she pulled Colly to her and just had to give her another hug.

Silas's father, Borden Livingstone, was more subdued than his wife, though it was possible that he had not spent the last few years waiting for this very day the way his wife had.

Colly recognised him as the man who had been with Silas at her father's funeral, and warmed to Borden Livingstone when he offered his condolences and apologised that he had not spoken to her then.

'Would you like something to drink first, or are you ready to eat?' Silas asked as they ambled into the drawing room.

'We'd better eat,' his mother declared, her eyes approvingly flicking from one flower arrangement to the other. 'I've hardly been able to eat a thing all day. I'd better get something solid down before I attempt anything alcoholic.'

Colly liked her mother-in-law. She was such a warm and natural person and Colly felt it would be difficult not to like her. She wished she could be as natural in return, and did try her very hardest so to be. But she was aware that she had to be on her guard; any small slip and she could see they would have to confess the truth.

Though as they chatted all through the first course, and enjoyed each other's company, so Colly did begin to feel a little more relaxed.

It was midway through the main course, however—Mrs

Varley having excelled herself with crispy roast duck in a black cherry sauce—that Colly realised she just could not afford to relax.

Paula Livingstone made some passing reference to the tropical bug Silas had picked up, and said how heartily relieved she had been to know that someone he might be serious about was going to collect him from the hospital and would look after him. 'Of course I didn't know then that you and Silas were married,' she went on warmly, with a happy glance at Colly's wedding band before going smilingly on, 'We very nearly met then, when I came to check on him—but you'd already left.'

Oh, grief, what could she say? Colly recalled that she had left the apartment before nine that morning—she had no idea how soon afterwards Silas's mother had arrived.

'I don't think Colly will mind me telling you—she's been having a few problems in connection with her father's will,' Silas slotted in smoothly. Colly glanced to him and supposed that, given the problems that had faced her when she had thought herself left out of her father's will, Silas was speaking only the truth.

'Oh, I'm so sorry, Colly.' Paula was instantly sympathetic. And, turning to her husband, 'I'm sure our legal advisers would be—'

'It's no longer a problem,' Silas informed her.

How could he say that when the consequences of the action she had taken when thinking herself homeless, jobless and penniless were still reverberating around her? And what consequences! For heaven's sake, unless she could think up something close to brilliant, she was going to have to share a bedroom with him tomorrow night!

'I'm so glad you've been able to resolve matters,' Paula said kindly.

'The house is being sold.' Colly, not wanting to think about anything to do with that trip to Dorset, was ready to chat about anything to keep her mind off it. 'It's a large house, with years of accumulated impediments to sort through. I've been spending most of my days there.'

'I shouldn't know where to start should we ever decide to sell our house,' Paula sympathised. 'Borden has so much clutter.'

'Clutter?' he came in, effecting to look amazed.

'I swear he's hoarded every engineering magazine that was ever published,' his wife replied. 'He has years and years of back issues.'

When Mrs Varley served the last course, Silas, with a look to Colly as if to seek her confirmation, a gesture that was purely for his parents' benefit, thanked Mrs Varley and said that they would see to everything else themselves. Colly thanked her too. In her view Mrs Varley was a first-class cook.

All in all it had been a happy meal, Colly considered. If feelings of guilt had come along and given her a nip every now and then, she hoped she had been too well mannered to let it show.

She did not feel she could breathe easy, though, until, with hugs and kisses and a very firm suggestion that she and Silas should dine with them before too long, they went to wave his parents off.

'Was that so bad?' Silas asked as they came back along the hall.

'Your parents are super,' she answered, adding coolly as they headed towards the kitchen, 'The guilt I shall have to live with.' They went into the kitchen and she owned she felt somehow on edge with Silas. 'But if you can get me out of another dinner I'd be glad.' Ready to tackle the remaining dishes, Mrs Varley having already loaded up the dishwasher, Colly began to fill the sink. 'I'll leave it fifteen minutes, then I'll be on my way,' she commented, thinking to wait until his parents were well clear.

She began to wash the pots and pans, but to her surprise Silas picked up a cloth and began to dry them. 'You could stay if you like?' he offered equably after some moments. She looked at him, startled, and caught a glimpse of his smile as he added, 'I've a spare bedroom. It wouldn't…'

She knew he had a spare bedroom; she had used it. And she would love to stay, but… Was love always about denial? 'I think it's enough that I shall have to put up with you tomorrow night,' she said sharply, fearful that her need to be with him might yet see her give in. But, since the subject was there, just crying out to be addressed, 'I—er…' she murmured, her voice already losing its sharp edge. She looked away from him. 'I suppose there's no chance I'll have a room of my own tomorrow night?'

She had to look at him again. She saw he was unsmiling, but she heard a note of sensitivity in his tones when, his glance gentle on her, he answered, 'I'm afraid, Colly, that is very unlikely.'

Her heartbeats suddenly started to thunder at his gentle look. And all at once—perhaps it was partly to do with the strain of the evening; she could not have said—she just knew she needed to be by herself.

'Hard-hearted Hannah's leaving you with the dishwashing *and* the drying,' she announced, taking her hands from the water and drying them.

She went into the drawing room, where she had left her small evening purse, and picking it up took out her car keys. She heard a sound and looked up to see that Silas had come to stand in the drawing room doorway.

She went towards him. He did not move out of her way, and even though her heart was thundering she managed to find a little acid to tell him bluntly, 'Might I suggest that as soon as you've done the dishes you go and get as much sleep as you can?' He raised a mocking eyebrow. 'And it might be an idea if you had a lie-in in the morning.'

'You reckon?' he drawled.

Oh, she did. She very much did. 'From where I'm viewing it, unless that room in Dorset has twin beds, it very much looks as if you're in for a very uncomfortable night tomorrow,' she said sweetly, adding for smiling good measure, 'Sleepless in a chair.'

He was not taken in by her phoney sweetness. Nor was he put out by what she had said either. But he managed, effortlessly, to take the fake smile off her face when, as nicely as you please, he enquired, 'Did I say that to you when you insisted on getting into bed with me that time?'

Speechlessly she glared at him. It had not been like that, and he knew it. But, having effectively silenced her syrupy tones, Silas stood away from the door to let her pass.

She was already on her way when, 'I'll call for you round about two,' he said, going to the door with her.

Don't bother, sprang to mind—but, against that, she loved the man; she knew she could not let him down.

CHAPTER EIGHT

THERE were five minutes to go before two o'clock on Saturday afternoon when Silas called for her. Colly was ready and waiting. Although inwardly she felt that she would never be ready.

She swallowed hard before she could open the door to him. And had to again remind herself of the lecture she had given herself about forgetting her guilt, her feelings that she was deceiving some octogenarian. She must see the other side of this coin. Think of Silas. He had not been thinking of himself when he had decided he must marry, but thinking of the good of the company, its workers and its shareholders. As he had said, his grandfather wanted to meet his wife and she—she was his wife.

She opened the door. 'Sorry to have kept you.' She apologised for her delay in answering his knock. Silas was casually dressed in trousers and shirt and she was basically simply pleased to see him. 'I'll just get my overnight bag,' she murmured.

Silas carried her bag to his car, and a minute or so later they were on their way. 'My mother rang to thank you for a wonderful evening,' he thought to mention.

Obviously he had made the appropriate excuses for her not being there. 'On reflection, I think the evening went off quite well,' she commented.

'My parents loved you,' Silas answered.

'Oh, don't!' she cried, guilt having another stab at her. 'They were ready to love any woman you married before they met me.' She told it as she saw it, knowing in her heart that

148

she would love to be a true daughter-in-law to Paula Livingstone. 'Your mother's so warm.'

'You've missed that,' he said softly, perceptively, and asked, 'How old were you when you lost your mother?'

'Eight,' she replied, but did not want to dwell on that. 'You will get us out of dining with your parents again, won't you?'

'You worry to much,' he said, which to her mind was no sort of an answer.

She fell silent, and as mile after mile sped by Silas seemed occupied with his own thoughts. Though he did think to ask after some while, 'Anything else worrying you, Colly?'

'Where would you like me to start?' she answered snappily. But was then instantly ashamed of herself. 'I'm sorry,' she apologised. 'All this is more my fault than yours.'

'What a sweetheart you are,' he replied, and her heart did a tiny kind of giddy flip—he had sounded as though he really meant it.

'I've been thinking only of myself and my guilt, but you too must be hating like blazes that you don't feel able to be open about our—er—relationship with your family.'

She did not know what she expected him to answer to that, but she was momentarily floored when, quite out of the blue, he quietly let fall, 'You know, Mrs Livingstone, I think I quite enjoy being married to you.'

Her mouth fell open in shock, and she was glad he had his eyes on the road in front. Silas quite enjoyed being married to her? A song began in her heart—until plain and utter common sense flooded in. Why wouldn't he enjoy being married to her? They were living apart. He had the marriage certificate he needed, but that was as far as his commitment went.

Which in turn had to mean that, of anyone he could have chosen to do a marriage deal with, he was happy he had made the right choice. Well, bully for him!

Realising she was getting nettled and uptight again—which

was no sort of mood to be in to meet her grandfather-in-law, Colly made a more determined effort.

'Uncle Henry phoned yesterday,' she said brightly.

'He'd read of our marriage?' Silas guessed. And, straight on the heels of that, 'You didn't tell him…?'

'Thank you for your confidence!' she snapped, but knew she was in the wrong and gave a heartfelt sigh. 'Why am I always apologising to you? I know, I know,' she went hurriedly on, 'I slipped up before with Tony Andrews. But I didn't with Uncle Henry.'

'Was he very put out?'

'He was very understanding, actually. I told him the apartment belonged to your grandfather, by the way. And,' she felt obliged to go on, 'that you go abroad from time to time, but that when you are home you sometimes stay at the apartment.'

'Have I made a liar of you?' he questioned with a kind glance.

'That's what you told me,' she defended. 'That you sometimes stay overnight.'

'Remind me to do it more often,' he responded dryly.

She laughed—this man did that to her.

Silas Livingstone Senior was tall, like all the Livingstone men. He had a thatch of white hair, was upright, and came out to greet them. He did not hug her, but after shaking hands with Silas took her hand warmly in his. His words were warm too, as he feasted his eyes on her, and demanded, 'How dare that grandson of mine run off and marry you without me there to wish you well?'

Colly smiled at him, a natural warm smile, as she replied, 'We didn't want to wait and we didn't want any fuss.' And, because they had done him out of attending his grandson's wedding, 'I'm sorry.'

'With a smile like that I'll forgive you,' he replied gallantly, and invited, 'Come in. Gwen's got the kettle boiling.'

Gwen, it appeared, was his housekeeper, a plump little lady

who had been with the Senior Livingstones for years. And Gwen it was who wheeled a trolley into the drawing room.

But it was Colly who poured the tea and, over tea and cake, accepted Grandfather Livingstone's regrets that he had not attended her father's funeral.

Colly realised that her father's funeral had not been all that many months after Silas Senior had lost his wife. And that, his age apart, perhaps he had not been emotionally up to attending a funeral.

'You knew my father?' she enquired.

'Not personally. But most people in the engineering world knew or had heard of him,' he answered, and spoke of several of her father's achievements.

Colly felt very proud, and suddenly realised that she felt quite relaxed. She was proud of Silas too, when he and his grandfather had a short conversation about something to do with engineering—all Greek to her—that cropped up as a side issue.

But, both men plainly thinking it not too polite to talk on a subject she could not join in, they swiftly abandoned the topic, only for her feeling of being relaxed to go plummeting when Grandfather Livingstone suggested to Silas, 'You'll want to freshen up, I expect. Your room's all ready for you. It's the one at the front.'

Oh, heavens! It was a large house, a house in its own grounds. But, as large as it was, there was no chance of their 'room' being a suite.

'We'll take our bags up, shall we, Colly?' Silas suggested easily, apparently aware which bedroom his grandfather referred to.

'Fine,' she answered, smiling, hoping her sudden feeling of tension was not showing to the elderly man who, she was fast realising, was thrilled that his grandson had married and brought his bride to see him.

Silas carried both their overnight bags up the stairs. She

was banking on twin beds. Wrong! As soon as the door was open she shot a speedy glance to the sleeping arrangements— it was a double bed.

As Silas stepped by her, and went to place their bags on the floor, so Colly stayed where she was. When thinking she might have to share a room with him she had been able to convince herself that, while preferring it to be otherwise, she would, for the sake of what they were about, be able to cope. But now, with the reality of it here, she did not feel convinced at all!

'What's wrong?' Silas had noticed that she seemed frozen over by the door.

'Nothing,' she answered stiltedly, her glance darting to the only padded chair in the room. She moved more into the room and Silas came and closed the bedroom door. When he un-expectedly placed his hands on her shoulders she jumped as though bitten.

'Nothing!' Silas scorned, turning her to face him. 'It looks like it!'

'Don't go on!' she snapped, pulling out of his hold.

If she had hoped he would leave it there, however, she discovered it was a forlorn hope. 'Look,' Silas began sternly, plainly not best pleased to have her so jumpy when he was anywhere near, 'as far as anyone knows you and I are married. But,' he went on, to lay it on the line, 'while I accept that you are a beautiful and desirable woman, you have to accept that I do not want to do anything that—in the long term— will bind you permanently to me.'

That well and truly did away with her tension. Not because of what he said, his attempt at reassurance, but because of his inference that she might give him half a chance should he try and test the water. 'As if—' she flared—who the devil did he think he was?

'So, whatever fears you have of anything happening between you and me,' he cut in before she could go for his jugular, 'forget it!'

She opened her mouth, ready with a few choice words, but with difficulty swallowed them down. 'Right!' she hurled at him, glaring at him. He stared back.

'Now what's wrong?' he demanded bluntly, his expression dark.

Let him whistle for an answer. But as she continued to glare stubbornly at him, so his dark expression suddenly cleared, and she knew she was not going to like what was coming even before it arrived. She didn't.

'Surely,' he began, 'you don't *want* anything to happen between us that will consummate—'

'Stop right there, Livingstone!' she erupted. 'I do not now, or ever...' Suddenly she ran out of steam. All at once she began to see the funny side of their non-argument—for what was there to argue about? Neither of them wanted the same thing. Her lips started to twitch, and while she became aware that his eyes were on her mouth she just had to tell him. 'In relation to your "What's wrong?" I suppose I'm just a touch miffed that you—or any man, given these circumstances— should be so immune to my charms.'

His lips twitched too, as she came to an end, and she guessed he appreciated her honesty when, honest himself, he took her in his arms and replied, 'Immune? I think you know better than that—don't you, Colly?'

She looked up at him, her heart pounding. 'So now we know where we stand?'

'Exactly,' he agreed, placed a light kiss on her lips and, his arms dropping to his sides, took a step back from her. 'Sing out if there's anything you need. I'll go and keep my grandfather company until you're ready to join us.'

Colly unpacked the few things she had brought with her after Silas had gone. She acknowledged that she felt better for what she could only think of as Silas's wading in to clear the air. Indeed, now that he was no longer in the room with her she began to wonder what all the fuss had been about. Silas had let her know point-blank that he wanted the state of their marriage to stay exactly as it was, and that she could sleep easy with him in the same room. But—a smile lit within her—it was nice to know that he was not totally immune to her.

She owned to feeling a touch apprehensive, however, when in the early evening she went down to dinner. But she discovered, with Silas there as a buttress and his grandfather being a man of courtesy and olde worlde charm, that she had no need to feel in the slightest apprehensive. The only small hiccup occurred—and she was sure that she was the only one who felt in any way awkward—when Grandfather Livingstone asked Silas, 'I don't suppose you've had time to check on the apartment recently?'

'I have,' Silas answered, having been there that very day. 'You've nothing to worry about there,' he assured him.

A short while later they left the dining room and returned to the drawing room, and Colly realised a little to her surprise, as the next hour ticked by, that all in all it had been a very pleasant evening.

When, during the conversation that followed in the next half an hour, she picked up that Silas's grandfather was usually in bed by ten-thirty, she thought the time might be right to make noises about retiring.

'I'll be up later,' Silas commented.

Nerves started to try and get a foothold again. 'I'll say goodnight, then.' She smiled as she got to her feet and both men stood.

Up in the bedroom she was to share with Silas, she blocked her mind to all save reliving the lecture he had given her: while not being immune to her, he had no desire to make theirs a full marriage.

On the plus side she discovered that her grandfather-in-law's household did not subscribe to the more modern duvet when it came to bedding. She showered and got into her nightdress and, leaving herself with sheets and a blanket, went and draped the over-large padded quilt over what she wincingly saw looked to be a not-very-comfortable chair. It still did not look very comfortable after she had draped the quilt over it. She added a pillow.

From there she went and switched on the bathroom light, and left the bathroom door ajar so Silas should have sufficient light to find his way around without banging into anything. Hopeful that she would be asleep before Silas came to bed, she put out the bedroom light and got into the big double bed. Just so that there should be no mistake, she opted to occupy the centre of the bed.

But so much for her hope to be asleep before Silas came up the stairs. She was still wide awake when, what seemed like hours later, she heard him at the door. She had her back to the bathroom her eyes closed, and was concentrating solely on making her breathing sound even when, almost silently, Silas came in, quietly closing the door after him.

If he knew that she was still awake he said nothing. She had nothing she wanted to say either. He must have taken her hint when he had seen the light from the bathroom, and did not turn on any other light. She heard him moving about, then, when the bathroom door closed, she opened her eyes to find the room in darkness.

Shortly afterwards there was light again, briefly. She closed her eyes, heard the light switch off, and knew that Silas was making his way to that not-too-comfortable-to-sleep-in chair. At least that was where she hoped he was making his way to; there would be all-out war if he thought he was sharing her bed!

It was a thought that, after an hour, or it might have been two, of listening to Silas trying to get his long length comfortable, she was having to review.

The chair creaked again as he once more adjusted his position, and she started to weaken, started to feel sorry for him. Just what had he done to deserve this? Nothing but try to do his best for the firm his grandfather had started.

Well, one sleepless night would not hurt him, argued her other self. He would probably have backache for a week, but… The chair creaked again as he attempted again to silently adjust his position.

'Oh, for goodness' sake!' she found she was erupting. 'Bring your pillow and that quilt over here and get on top of the bed! Feet my way up!' she ordered as an afterthought, and shunted over so he should have ample room.

She heard him move, and wished she had kept quiet, and was not at all appeased when, his voice near, 'For you, I bought a pair of pyjamas,' he informed her.

'I don't care if you're wearing a suit of armour!' she snapped. 'You're still sleeping with your feet my way up.'

She heard his low laugh and could not deny that all at once there was a bubble of laughter in her too. Sternly, she repressed it. Then felt the bed go down. Silas, sleeping his head to her toes, had joined her.

Though what sleep he got she did not know. For herself she was so overly conscious of him next to her she just could not sleep. He was so near, so dear—oh, think of something else, do.

Somewhere around dawn she felt him leave the bed. Either he was an early riser or he could not sleep either. She guessed it was the former. She heard the bathroom door close and surmised he was ready to shower and dress and start his day.

She closed her eyes and at last managed to get some sleep. But she did not sleep for too long; some inbuilt 'manners' alarm was there to remind her that she was a guest and that guests had certain duties. One of which was not to be late should breakfast be being served at some rigid time.

She sat up, hugging the sheet and blanket to her as she took

a tentative look around. She relaxed. As she had supposed,
Silas was up and out. Following suit, she slipped the fallen
narrow shoulder-strap of her nightdress back in place and left
the bed ready to take a shower.

She headed for the bathroom, wondering at what time they
would leave. If— She opened the bathroom door and her
thoughts, her body, everything, became motionless. She stared
stunned, immobile. She had thought—no, not even thought,
had just been certain that Silas had vacated the bathroom ages
ago. She had thought she had been asleep for an hour or so—
but realised that she could not have been asleep anywhere
near that long, that her only sleep must have been the briefest
of catnaps. Because the bathroom was not empty. Silas was
in there. And—he was stark naked!

He was sideways on to her, half turned from her as he stood
before the large mirror, having obviously just finished shav-
ing. He had turned his head as the bathroom door opened,
and simultaneously her yelp of 'Ooh!' had rent the air as her
stunned glance took in his long length of leg, the well-
muscled thigh, his right buttock, not to mention part of his
broad naked back.

Then her eyes met his and scorching colour seared her skin.
She was unsure who moved first, but, not lingering to have a
debate about it, Colly found release from her rooted immo-
bility and spun urgently about.

She had taken a couple of steps back into the bedroom but
had still not got her head together, being unsure what to do—
whether to take a dive back under the bedcovers or, totally
unnerved as she was, what.

She stood there, crimson, striving hard to tell herself not to
make an issue of it, that Silas was more sinned against than
sinning. As far as he had been concerned she was fast asleep;
the last thing he'd expected was that she would barge in and
invade his privacy.

Then she heard him come and stand behind her. 'This gets worse!' she uttered croakily.

'I didn't think I looked so very dreadful stripped off,' Silas answered, plainly endeavouring to make light of it. But she could find no humour in the situation.

'Don't!' she said huskily. 'I didn't know you were in there!' she explained hurriedly. And she did not know just where she was when from behind his arms came around to the front of her in a loose hold. She glanced jerkily down and was overwhelmingly relieved to see from his silk-clad arms that he must have hastily donned a robe. 'I thought you'd showered and gone.'

'I rather think I know that,' he said to the top of her head. And, taking the blame totally on himself, 'Last time I looked you were sound away. But even so, bearing in mind that there's no lock on the bathroom door, I should have hung a note on the handle or something.'

'It—doesn't matter,' she replied.

His arms firmed a little around her. She was not sure that he did not drop a light kiss to the top of her head. Wishful thinking, she realised, and also realised all at once that she was clad in a thin shortie nightdress, and that, since she could feel the heat of his body, possibly all Silas had on was the fine silk robe.

She went to move away but his arms held her, and in all honesty she would by far prefer to stay just where she was. Soon they would be back in London, her closeness with him over; she needed these moments to treasure.

'You've been brilliant, Colly,' Silas said softly, bending to her ear. 'Just a few more hours,' he promised, 'and then we can say goodbye to the weekend.'

Just a few more hours! She wanted to stay like this for ever. 'I never wanted to make a fuss,' she replied, and whether he went to give her a bit of a hug or if she was just obeying some compulsion she could not have said—but Colly moved and leaned back against him.

He did not push her away from him, and the side of his face was almost touching the side of her face. 'You've been wonderful,' he applauded her.

Oh, help her, she was starting to feel all wobbly. She strove for levity. 'Is that what you say to all the girls after you've slept with them?' she asked with a light laugh.

He turned her then. His hands coming to her arms, he turned her to face him. 'You're special,' he replied, his own tone light.

Colly smiled, recalling the time when she had queried whether, married to her, he might want to marry someone else. She'd have to be more than a little extra-special, he had replied. 'Careful,' she warned. 'When you get to ''extra-special'' I'm bailing out.'

For answer Silas stared down at her, his dark blue eyes fixed on her green ones. And for ageless moments they just seem to stare wordlessly at each other. Then suddenly she felt him drawing her that little bit closer.

She thought it might be a good idea to resist. Only then his lips were over hers, gently over hers, warm over hers, and she had no hope of resisting him. She loved him. Why should she resist?

He broke his kiss. She tried to find her voice. But her brain seemed word-starved, and all she could think to say was a shy 'Good morning.'

He laughed. 'Good morning, wife,' he said, and seemed to so enjoy calling her his wife that any logic that tried to penetrate, to tell her nonsense, just did not stand a chance of getting through.

'You've got a very nice mouth, Mr Livingstone,' she thought to mention.

'You have my permission to kiss it, should its niceness become too much for you,' he suggested.

Logic at that point tried to get a toe-hold—this was not the way this weekend was supposed to go. But logic was a cold bedfellow, and she would much rather take her husband up on his offer.

Of their own volition her arms went round him. She felt his warmth, the cleanness of him. And she just had to kiss him. She stretched up invitingly. Obligingly he bent down, and responded fully.

They broke apart. Feeling a little breathless, she stared at him. 'I...' she said, but could not go on. Because what she wanted to tell him was that she loved him—and whatever else her mixed-up brain patterns were confusing her with, she somehow knew that to tell him that would be the height of folly.

'You...?' he prompted, his wonderful mouth quirking upwards at the corners.

'I—um—think I'm feeling a touch confused,' she confessed.

He smiled gently at her, as if understanding. 'Would another kiss help, do you suppose?'

He had to be joking! It was those kisses that were partly responsible! But, even though she must refuse his most tempting offer, she was finding she just could not. 'I shouldn't like you to think me greedy,' she murmured—and said no more.

How could she? Silas had drawn her to him again. Held fast against his heart, Colly was no longer thinking but was feeling, enjoying, and in utter seventh heaven as the man she loved with her whole heart kissed her not once but many times.

And she adored his kisses, returned his kisses without restraint. Adored the way his fingers strayed through her long dark hair, the way his hands cupped her face. The way he transferred his hand to hold her in his arms.

'Silas!' She murmured his name when somehow, and she

had no clue how she had got there, all at once she found she was against a wall and Silas was leaning to her.

'You're...?' he began, his voice all kind of gravelly. 'I'm not alarming you?' he rephrased.

'Do you want me?' she asked huskily.

'Oh, sweet, innocent love,' he murmured, to thrill her. And, with a smile, 'Yes, I think you could say that,' he breathed, and as they moulded together so, wide-eyed, she stared at him.

'Oh!' she gasped.

'I'm—worrying you?' he asked, pulling back.

She shook her head. 'It's just I—um—think my—education in certain matters has just gone up another notch.' And as he grinned, seeming delighted with her, she wanted again to feel his wanting body against her, and pushed her wanting body against him.

'Colly!' he breathed, and kissed her, and it was such a kiss that she knew then that she was leaving the nursery slopes of lovemaking.

'Oh, Silas!' she cried, and wound her arms about him, loving every movement, every whispered kiss, as he traced tender kisses down the side of her throat, his hands caressing her all but naked shoulders.

She held on to him when, with one hand holding her close, his other hand caressed round to capture one of her breasts. A fire of such longing was leaping within her—she wanted more.

'Oh!' she sighed, as his sensitive fingers played and teased at the hardened tip of her breast. And again, 'Oh!' she cried, on a wanting kind of sound, when he bent his head and through the thin material of her nightdress gently pressed his lips to her breast, before once more claiming her lips.

Silas kissed her with long, slow, wonderful kisses, and his hands strayed behind her, to hold and caress her back, her waist, her buttocks.

When his searching hands found their way beneath her

nightdress, and those warm caressing fingers touched her naked buttocks, and he intimately pulled her to him, Colly
thought she would faint.

She kissed him because she needed to. But her nightdress
was all at once a hindrance. 'Do we need this?' Silas asked
softly, his fingers on the thin cotton, her only covering.

And belatedly modesty—she could only afterwards suppose
because she was as near naked as made no difference—suddenly woke up with a vengeance.

'No—I mean, yes.'

She did not know what she meant, other than that the idea
of standing totally unclothed before him was completely alien
to her—she just could not do it. This was all new ground to
her, and love him quite desperately though she did, want him
quite desperately as she did, there was just something in her
that screamed out no. Perhaps it was something in her up-
bringing, some shyness at being the way she was with a man
for the first time in her life. She just did not know.

But, 'No, I can't,' she said, panicking, swallowing hard, the
idea of standing naked in front of Silas an entire anathema to
her.

Silas, his skin slightly flushed—so she guessed her own
face must be on fire—stared disbelievingly at her. 'You don't
want to make love with me?' he questioned throatily, his
hands falling away as he put some space between their two
bodies, his eyes searching hers as he stepped back.

She did not mean that at all! Her whole body was throbbing
with her need for him. But suddenly, despite the intimacy they
had been sharing, and maybe because Silas had stepped back
and was no longer touching her, she all at once hit a hard
impenetrable wall of that belated and unwanted modesty. She
just could not find the words to tell him, Yes, I need you, yes,
I want you, please take me.

Dumbly she shook her head. Confusion? She was drowning
in it. So why did her voice sound so composed, so apart,

when, after taking a step to one side, 'Had you finished with the bathroom?' she heard a female stranger enquire.

She risked a glance at Silas. He was looking as if he could not believe it either. But there was no way he was going to force himself on her. He took another step away from her. 'My stars, you're a cool one!' he gritted.

Cool? If only he knew. 'I'll take that as a yes, then, shall I?' the female stranger asked. Colly went while she could, lest she should throw her arms around him and beg him to understand that no man had ever seen her naked, that while she was not ashamed of her body she seemed to have a hang-up about nudity.

They were silent on the journey back to London. Colly had plenty to think about, and Silas appeared to have much on his mind. Work, most likely, she assumed, quite certain that a man of his sophistication would not bother to dwell on what had happened between them.

She did not want to dwell on it either. She had stayed in the bathroom for a positive age after she had left him. He had not stayed around, though, and hadn't been in the bedroom when she'd eventually gone in. What, after all, had there been to stay around for? They had shared a few heady moments—heady—understatement of the year—but he had not tried to stop her when, misunderstanding her, 'No, I can't,' he had let her go.

Something she realised he must now be more than pleased about. He had not the smallest wish to cement their marriage, and was probably at this very moment thanking his lucky stars that when desire had sparked, though he had initially only meant to comfort her, she—so he had thought—had called a halt.

Well, she was glad too, she thought sniffily, because to make love with each other just was not in their contract. Oh, stop thinking about it, do.

'Are you all right?' The terse question cut through the strained atmosphere in the car.

Big of him to ask! No, she was not all right. Far from it. 'Why wouldn't I be?' she enquired, her voice proudly off-hand.

Silence settled in the car once more. She supposed he looked as grim as he sounded, but it was for sure she was not going to look at him to find out.

'I'll take half the blame if you'll take the other half,' he offered grimly.

'That's the least you can do!' she retorted, and, just so he should know, 'And if you don't mind I'd prefer not to discuss it.' She could feel herself getting all hot and bothered even before they went any further.

A grunt was her answer. Good. She switched her thoughts back to how she had discovered an unknown talent for acting when she had finally gone down the stairs to join Silas and his grandfather. Or maybe it had been just good manners in front of the elderly gentleman. But somehow or other over the next few hours she had managed to chat and smile with both men as though nothing out of the ordinary had so recently taken place in her life.

And when, shortly after lunch, Silas had said they should be on their way, and his grandfather had come out to the car with them and had commented, 'It has done my heart good to see you, Colly,' it had seemed natural that they should hold hands and kiss cheeks. Just as Silas had started up the car, 'Come again, *soon*,' he had urged.

If she had anything to do with it, that would never happen.

'Thank you for coming with me,' Silas said formally when he'd parked outside the apartment block and they got out of the car.

I wouldn't have missed it for the world, she thought acidly. 'That's all right,' she muttered, and felt as fed-up as Silas sounded.

'I'll bring your bag in.'

No way! She'd had one close encounter with him. She did not want him in her sitting room, where they might exchange verbal fisticuffs. 'No need!' she answered sharply. And, feeling close to tears suddenly, 'See you!' she mumbled. Taking her overnight bag, she went quickly from him before he should tell her, Not if I see you first.

She went to bed that night with her spirits at rock bottom. And, after a dreadful for the most part sleepless night, got out of bed on Monday morning with her spirits still down on the floor.

The situation, she felt, was hopeless. She and Silas could not have a proper marriage even should she want one—and it was for definite that he didn't—so what was the point of them staying married?

Well, she did not have to think about that very deeply. She knew the answer to that one. But from where she was viewing it, to get divorced from each other would suit her quite well.

Were they divorced then it would put an end to his parents inviting them to dinner and other family functions—which she could see might well crop up. And while Colly had truly liked Silas's parents, and while she would have loved to be a part of Silas's family, how could she be?

Look what had happened at the weekend? 'Come again, *soon*,' Grandfather Livingstone had urged when they were leaving. How could she go back there again with Silas?

She could not. Remembering how everything had got out of hand—to make love had never been in their agreement—Colly knew she dared not risk that again. Yet for how long could Silas stall his parents, his grandfather?

But, when to divorce seemed to be the only answer, Colly knew that she could not divorce Silas unless she wanted his feckless cousin to ultimately be in charge of Livingstone Developments and thereby ruin the work of three generations of Livingstones.

Colly knew she could not do that to Silas. She wished that she did not love him so much, and knew then that she should never have married him. But she also knew that she was glad she had known him. When all was said and done, he had never asked her to fall in love with him. And after the short way he had been with her on the drive home it was obvious he would be totally appalled at any such idea of them being any closer than they were. He did not want that sort of involvement.

The day dragged wearily on, with every hour seeming like ten. But, to show that she was not the only one in low spirits, Rupert Thomas phoned her around five that afternoon and sounded really out of sorts.

Colly had been tempted not to answer the phone when it rang. But it was then that common sense, pure and simple, stepped in to scornfully prod. Did she really think that after the dozen or so unfriendly words she and Silas had exchanged on the drive home it might be him calling for a chat? Get real!

'What are you doing tonight?' Rupert asked, his tone glum.

He'd been dumped again? 'Nothing in particular,' she replied, realising that tomorrow she was going to have to hide her own feelings while she listened, chapter and verse, to Rupert's latest tragedy.

'Can you have dinner with me?' he wanted to know.

She'd had dinner with him before—he was good company when he was up. 'Any particular reason?' she enquired. He was a pain when he was down, but he was a friend.

'You'll never believe it!' he launched in at her invitation. 'That wretched Averil Dennis has given me the elbow!'

'Oh, I'm sorry,' Colly sympathised, and for the next five minutes listened to a catalogue of the said Averil's faults.

'I badly need someone to talk to,' Rupert said as he came to an end. 'Say you'll have dinner with me?'

Colly was about to remind him that she would be seeing

him at the gallery tomorrow, when he would be able to talk his little cotton socks off, but abruptly, before she could say a word, changed her mind. What are you doing tonight? he had asked. Well, she wasn't doing anything tonight. Nor was she doing anything tomorrow night, or the night after that, nor, for that matter, any night in the foreseeable future. And it just was not good enough!

'I'd love to have dinner with you, Rupert,' she answered. And, forcing a bright note, 'Where are we going?' she asked, determined to rise above her down feeling. 'The White Flamingo?' It was one of his favourite haunts.

'Hmm—I thought I'd take you somewhere a bit more up-market than that,' he replied. 'Averil introduced me to this place. I'll pick you up about seven.'

'I'll be ready.' Colly guessed that Rupert was half hoping that Averil would be dining at that establishment, so he could either stick his nose in the air and ignore her—or introduce her to Averil as though she were his latest.

Colly did not mind. Rupert had lived and enjoyed a hard life, and though he was forty looked fifty, but he was harmless, and most of the time quite amusing, and besides, she was fond of him.

He was on time, and it was all Averil from the word go. He plainly had not read of her marriage to Silas, Colly realised, and realised too that, with the heartless Averil taking up central position in his head, he most likely would not have commented on it even if he had known.

Whether or not he knew of her marriage, however, suddenly became irrelevant. Because as Rupert drove on Colly was all at once filled with a feeling of apprehension. She had to be wrong. She had to! But, if she were not wrong, Rupert was heading for the same hotel where she had dined with Silas that night he had made that amazing suggestion that they marry!

'Rupert, I—' broke from her urgently when he halted his

car at the hotel. But he was getting in a fluster over a parking space that someone else was trying to grab, and either did not hear her or assumed she was taking him to task for being so bullish.

She calmed down. What did it matter? This hotel might have a favourite dining room for Averil, but it did not necessarily follow that it was a favourite for Silas too. For goodness' sake, there were dozens of restaurants in London! What about that restaurant Tony Andrews had taken her to that night Silas had come up to their table? Perhaps that was his favourite eating establishment.

Telling herself not to be ridiculous, Colly nevertheless scanned the dining room as she and Rupert went in. Then she realised that Rupert had been doing the same thing, though in his case he seemed disappointed that the object of his search was not dining there that night. For herself, Colly could not have said how she felt. She did not want to eat here. She knew well how idiotic she was being, but to her it was their place, hers and Silas's.

She was all tensed up, she knew that, and as it was relatively early she supposed Silas could still walk in—but did she want to see him again? Oh, to blazes with it—she positively ached to see him again.

'So I drove her home...' Rupert was saying. Colly tried to concentrate. '...and accidentally...' She was sitting where she could see the dining room door. It opened, and a tall dark-haired man came in; her heart thundered, then quietened. It was not Silas. '...think about that?' Rupert ended.

'Er—unfortunate,' Colly attempted.

And discovered she had said the right thing when Rupert took up, 'I'll say it was unfortunate! Averil swore I did it on purpose, but I...'

And so it went on through dinner. Colly tried not to look at the door every two minutes, and was glad to find she needed to make very little input as Rupert warmed to his 'heartless Averil' theme.

'...had enough?' he asked.

Colly felt out on a limb again, and hoped he was asking if she'd had sufficient to eat. 'That was a super meal,' she replied.

'We'll have coffee in the lounge, shall we?' he asked.

The lounge—where she and Silas had drunk coffee that night... Oh, Silas.

Not waiting for her answer, Rupert stood up. It was still early, not yet nine o'clock, but as they made their way to the lounge area so Colly felt she would much prefer to go home.

Less than a minute later she was wishing that she had said as much. Because as she and Rupert entered the lounge, so her eyes were immediately drawn to a good-looking dark-haired man seated, coffee-cups on the table before him, in deep conversation with a most attractive blonde!

Silas! Colly's spirits rapidly rose—only to hit the floor with an almighty crash. She had spent a good part of the evening watching every tall male who had come through the dining room door, whereas Silas was so engrossed with his coffee-drinking companion that he did not even look up when the lounge door opened.

Though even as a sick feeling battered Colly, and jealousy seared every part of her, Silas did take a moment to glance away from the blonde. His eyes met Colly's. She saw his glance go to her companion—he did not look too well pleased. All in less than two seconds, as he started to rise, so Colly was turning about and whispering to Rupert, 'I need to get out of here!'

She went speedily, and Rupert, to his credit, did not argue but followed her out. 'Feeling queasy?' he asked as he followed her to where he had parked his car.

Colly was too churned up to tell anything but the truth. 'I've just seen someone I don't want to see,' she said, though she wondered, as green barbs still pierced her, if it was not so much Silas she did not want to see, but Silas with another woman.

'Oh, I know that picture,' Rupert replied, and, as if fully understanding, 'Let's get going.'

Colly tried to remember her manners as Rupert drew up outside the apartment block. She had done him out of his coffee, and knew she should invite him in so she should make him a cup. But somehow she had not got the heart.

'Thank you for a lovely dinner,' she said instead, glad that Rupert had settled the account for their meal in the dining room, rather than leave it until after they'd had their coffee.

'It was good, wasn't it?' he replied, the defecting Averil having in no way affected his appetite, and, as Colly went to leave his car, 'See you tomorrow,' he said. 'I'll wait here until you get inside.'

Colly opened the outer door, turned and waved to him, and then went to the apartment. And she had thought she had been down before! She tried desperately hard to raise her spirits, but all she could see was Silas, deep in conversation with the pretty blonde.

Perhaps he was asking her to be wife number two, Colly thought with sour humour. But this was not a laughing matter. She hated feeling the way she did, and she hated him that he could make her feel that way.

She went and had a shower and got ready for bed. But sleep was light years away, so she returned to the sitting room—just as the phone started to ring.

Silas? As if! He'd got better things to do than remember he had a wife, she fumed sniffily. Rupert, then? Was she in the mood for more 'What Averil did'? Don't be mean. Rupert could not help it if he had a penchant for women who usually got their goodbyes in first.

She picked up the phone. 'Does he know you're not in line for a sugar-daddy?' Silas snarled grittily.

Shock, pleasure and hate fought for precedence. Jealousy romped in and flattened them all. 'Still keeping to your wedding vows, Livingstone?' she flew, and immediately wanted to bite out her tongue. Had she sounded jealous? Had Silas, shrewd, clever Silas, picked up that jealous tone? she wondered fearfully.

Whatever, there was a definite pause—but only so he could control his irritation with her, she quickly realised, when evenly, coolly, he had the nerve to ask, 'I wonder, Colly, if you'd care to have dinner with me tomorrow?'

And that made her mad! Furious! She just could not believe it! Only a little over an hour ago, definitely not more than that, he had been in deep conversation with a blonde! He was probably still *with* the blonde, Colly fumed, and that thought caused her fury to soar to volcanic proportions. Had he just excused himself from her to make this phone call? Was he still in that hotel with his blonde?

Vesuvius blew. *'Dinner!'* Colly exploded. 'I was thinking more of *divorcing* you than dining with you!' With that she slammed down the phone—and promptly burst into tears.

CHAPTER NINE

COLLY was at once ashamed. She dried her eyes and wondered where all that bad temper had come from. Oh, how could she have been so awful to Silas? She had never used to have such a temper.

She sighed as she realised that her emotions had been having a fine old time with her just recently. Well, ever since she had met Silas, in actual fact.

Although, on reflection, perhaps to some extent she had stepped on the roller-coaster of emotional upheaval starting with the shock at the unexpected death of her father.

Tears spurted to her eyes again. Tears she could not control ran unchecked down her cheeks. What with everything happening so fast—her father dying, followed by Nanette so soon as good as throwing her out of her home—Colly felt as if she had never properly mourned her father.

She again dried her tears, her thoughts on Silas and how he had found a solution to her problems—and his problems too, it had to be remembered. Oh, why had she to go and fall in love with him?

Tears pricked her eyes again, but this time she held them back. It was not the smallest good crying because she wanted Silas. She could not have him because he preferred blondes.

Why had he phoned? She acknowledged that she did not much care for his 'sugar-daddy' remark. But why had Silas asked her to have dinner with him? She guessed he had not been too pleased with her remark about divorcing him. But—

Her thoughts stopped right there when suddenly someone came knocking at her door. Silas! Or one of her neighbours? Silas—no! She'd got Silas on the brain. A neighbour, then?

Whoever. She was not going to answer the door. She was

172

not fit to be seen. Her eyes were most likely pink-rimmed
from crying, and in any case she was in her nightdress and
wrap and ready for bed.

If it were a neighbour who had seen a line of light under
her door she would see them tomorrow and plead she'd had
a headache. Were it Silas, then... Her breath caught—somebody was unlocking her door! Somebody—*was coming in*!

Silas had a key! In an instant she was on her feet, wanting
to run, wanting to hide. But too late. As cool as you like,
closing the door behind him, Silas was strolling into the sitting
room.

Her reaction was immediate. In the absence of being able
to hide, she turned her back on him. And, finding a snappy
note, antagonistically suggested, 'Would you very much mind
leaving? You're invading my personal space!' As if she
thought that would work.

'We need to talk,' Silas retorted sharply.

'You sound as though you would rather quarrel than talk!'
She stayed in there to erupt, still keeping her back to him.

'I don't—' he began, and to her dismay, plainly not a man
who enjoyed talking to someone's back, he came round to the
front of her '—want—' he added, but as she stared down at
the carpet so he halted, a hand all at once under her chin,
tilting her head up so he should see into her face. Abruptly
he left what he had been about to say. 'You've been crying!'
he accused.

'So?' she answered defiantly.

'Why?' he wanted to know. And, soon there with his conclusion, 'Who was that man you were with?' And, aggres-
sively, before she could answer, 'Did he—?'

'No, he didn't!' she replied heatedly. 'That was Rupert.'

'From the gallery?'

'Look, Silas, I'm ready for bed, and—'

'I'll wait if you want to go and get dressed,' he cut in.

That stopped her in her tracks, and some of her defiance
faded. 'You really do want to talk,' she commented.

There was a determined look about him, she noticed, but

his tone had lost its sharp edge when he asked, 'Why were you crying, Colly?'

She shrugged. 'A mixture of things, I suppose.' Silas waited. And when she did not want to tell him, most definitely did not want to tell him, she found she was going on, 'I never used to have a temper—then there I was yelling at you. Then…'

'You're saying that I'm the cause for your tears?' he asked, seeming not to like that idea one tiny bit.

'I think you're in there somewhere,' she understated. 'Probably the trigger,' she admitted. Having said so much, she felt she had to concede that. No way, though, was he going to know that he was the larger part of why she had given way to tears. 'Anyhow, with everything sort of exploding in my face, so to speak, I suddenly started to realise that, what with one thing and another, I never properly mourned my father when he died.'

'Your tears were for him?' Silas murmured, his tone so gentle she really had to protest.

'Don't go nice on me. You'll have me blubbering again!' she cried in alarm. But, gaining some control, added smartly, 'And if we're going to have a row, I prefer to—'

'I don't want to row with you,' Silas cut in. And, his voice now more matter-of-fact than anything, 'Things have sort of—got out of hand between us. I think,' he went on carefully, 'we should take time out to talk matters through.'

'It's nearly eleven o'clock!' she objected, just a little worried about where this talk would take them.

'You needn't go to the gallery tomorrow,' Silas decreed.

'Rupert will be thrilled,' she replied, but couldn't help being a touch pleased that Silas should remember that Tuesday was her gallery day.

'Shall we sit down?' he asked.

'This is going to take that long?' she queried as he led her over to the sofa and sat down beside her.

'As long as it takes,' he answered, as if—heedless of the fact he had to go to work tomorrow—he intended to stay all night if need be, until they had talked everything through. Colly was not sure that she wanted an in-depth discussion with Silas, when any unwary word she might utter might give him a hint of how she felt about him. 'You had dinner with him tonight?' Silas asked, which to her mind was hardly a subject for in-depth discussion.

'Rupert was feeling low. His latest girlfriend has decided she's seen enough of him for a while—Rupert likes to bend my ear on such occasions.'

'Some of your tears were for him?'

If she were honest she would have to say that, save thinking it might be him when her telephone had rung, she had not given Rupert another thought once his car had driven away. But, as that dreadful green-eyed monster gave her a nip, 'I don't remember seeing you in the dining room?' she remarked lightly, knowing without a question of a doubt that he had not been in the hotel dining room while she had been there.

'We didn't have a meal,' he replied. 'Come to think of it, apart from a sandwich earlier, I believe I completely missed out on dinner.'

'Didn't you feed her?' Oh, damn.

An alert light came to his eyes. 'You're not—jealous, Colly?' he asked, which did not surprise her in the slightest. She had heard that jealous note in her voice too. It would have been a miracle if he hadn't picked it up.

'*Pfff!*' she scorned, to bluff being the only way. 'I may be your wife, Livingstone, but I draw the line at having to be jealous as well.' Who was she—the blonde? And what, since eleven o'clock at night was probably early for Silas, was he doing here with her and not the blonde? 'Er—she looked very nice?' Colly found she was fishing anyway.

'She is,' he replied, and Colly wished she had not bothered. She was not sure she wanted to know any more when Silas went on, 'I was hoping to see you tonight when Naomi rang and asked if I would meet her. She was upset—'

'I don't really need to know about this,' Colly cut in coolly—now the name Naomi would haunt her for evermore.

'What did you want to talk about, Silas?' she managed to hold on to her cool note to enquire.

Silas looked at her levelly, either not liking her tone or wondering where to start. Since he never seemed at a loss for words, she doubted it was the latter.

Then his chin suddenly jutted, and his tone was totally uncompromising. 'I don't want to talk about divorce, that's for sure,' he said harshly.

And she immediately felt mean. Instantly she realised that he had every right to be angry that she had said she was thinking of divorcing him. 'I'm sorry, Silas. It was unfair of me to say, even in temper, that I was thinking of divorce.' For heaven's sake, she had known in advance that he would date other women. They were both free to date other people. 'It was particularly unfair when I knew you needed our marriage for the sake of the company. Will you—'

'This has nothing to do with the company!' he cut in grimly.

Colly stared at him. She was missing something here. 'We're... You... You're not here to talk about divorce?' she queried, trying to catch up. 'And this has nothing to do with the business?'

'Neither,' he agreed. But as she continued to stare at him, so she saw that his eyes seemed watchful on her.

'I—see,' she said slowly. But then had to confess, 'No, I don't.'

There was silence for several seconds before slowly, deliberately, he said, 'Marriage, Colly. I want to talk to you about our marriage.'

Marriage? Their marriage? They had not got a marriage. Not really, they hadn't. What they had was just a piece of paper, a certificate that united them. 'Our marriage?' she began to question. 'In relation to your family, you mean, and future meet—' Her voice tailed off. Silas was shaking his head.

'Our marriage in relation to—us,' he corrected.

'Oh,' she mumbled, while her heart pounded, as it did most

times when he was near. 'You're referring to what you said—about things sort of getting out of hand between us?' she dared bravely.

There was a hint of a smile about his mouth. 'It hasn't gone at all as I planned it,' he admitted.

'So much for forward planning.' She added her hint of a smile to his—he seemed encouraged.

'It seemed such a good idea at the start,' he confessed. 'You get your career and I got to keep long-term charge of the business. Only...' He hesitated.

'Only?' Colly prompted. It was odd. Silas was always so sure of what he was about, but if she did not know better she would say he was—nervous. Don't be ridiculous!

'Only at the outset the idea seemed flawless. I looked at it from every possible angle—or so I thought. And the more I thought about it, the more to marry you seemed the perfect solution—for you and for me. On my part, as suitable as you were, it wasn't as if I'd got to live with you.'

Thanks! 'A perfect solution, as you've said,' Colly murmured, striving not to sound sour.

'So I thought,' he agreed. 'But then events began to go off-plan.' Too true they had! Leave alone their personal involvement, he had been obliged, because of her 'letting the cat out', to introduce her to his family. 'They were never intended to go the way they did. Nor,' he added, his eyes on hers, 'did I ever expect I could feel the way I started to feel.'

'Oh,' Colly mumbled again. 'You—um—started to feel—um—differently—about something?' Now she was the one who was feeling nervous. What the Dickens did 'feel the way I started to feel' mean?

For answer, Silas stretched out a hand and took a hold of one of hers. Oh, help. Her heart did not merely pound, it thundered.

'You have to understand, Colly, that I'm a hard-headed businessman. Very little gets in the way of that.' She was not sure she believed that; not when it came to his family, she didn't. She had seen his respect for his father and his grandfather, his fond indulgence and also respect for his mother. 'But there we are, not even married yet, when here in this very room, on your first visit, you're getting all sparky when you think I'm doubting your honesty.' He paused. 'And there am I,' he resumed, 'experiencing a feeling of interest that shouldn't be there.'

Her eyes widened. 'Interest—in me?' she queried faintly.

He nodded. 'I scoffed at the very idea, of course.'

'Of course,' she agreed firmly.

'I scoffed again when I discovered I was not too keen on you dating other men.'

Her throat went dry. 'Well, you would, wouldn't you?' she murmured, which meant absolutely nothing, but gave her a chance to get her breath back.

He gave her hand a small shake. 'Colly,' he said, his dark blue eyes fixed on her wide green ones, 'I'm doing my best here to be restrained, but you've got me so that I don't know where the blazes I am.' Her eyes went saucer-wide. She'd got him so...! 'What I'm trying to tell you—hell, give me a tough board meeting any day—is that I have grown to l—care for you.'

'You haven't!' she denied instinctively. Then, because she wanted to believe it, 'Have you?' she asked huskily.

He did not answer for a moment or two. But, every bit as smart as she knew him to be, he had soon sifted through her brief reply. And, after another moment to check he had worked it out correctly, 'From what I've learned and know about you, I'd say you wouldn't ask "Have you?" if you weren't interested in knowing more.'

Oh, heavens! 'I—er—um—feel a bit on shaky ground here,' she confessed, and was rewarded with a smile.

'I know all about that shaky ground!' he said softly. 'And I'm trying with all I have not to rush you.'

'I remember once thinking that you were a man who liked things done yesterday,' she brought out of nowhere as nerves well and truly started to bite.

'But not now. Not here and now,' Silas took up. 'I don't

want to upset or worry you. Which is why I'm doing my best to take this slowly.'

She did not know what he meant. Why he thought she might feel rushed, or worried, or upset, so she stayed with what he had—astonishingly—so far said.

'You said you had grown to c-care for me?'

'I have, and I do,' he answered without hesitation. 'I wasn't supposed to. I did not want to. To care for you had no part in my plan. Yet there am I, on the day we marry, no less, kissing you—albeit briefly—and not because of the occasion but because I had to.'

Colly gaped at him. This couldn't be happening! 'I thought you kissed me because of people watching,' she whispered, with what breath she could find.

He shook his head in denial. 'It just came over me. I can see now that it was the first stirrings of starting to care for you.' Colly was still getting used to that when he went on, 'Naturally I, in my superior wisdom, denied any such nonsense.'

'Naturally,' she agreed, still feeling a touch breathless.

'So why are you in my head so much?'

'I am?'

'Even when I'm in tough board meetings,' he confirmed.

She stared at him incredulously. 'Heavens!' she said faintly.

'Several times I've had to control the urge to come and see you,' he surprised her by admitting. 'Just to check you were settled in all right—not for any other reason, obviously.'

'Why else?' she managed chokily.

'So I had mixed feelings when you wrote about your inheritance. At least it gave me a bona fide reason to call and see you.'

'Oh!' escaped her, but she was still too stunned to do more than sit tight—and hope.

'I decided I wouldn't come and see you again,' Silas revealed. Hope took on a dull sheen. 'But you were in my head so much,' he went on, to shoot her up to the high end of the see-saw she was on. 'Even when I landed up in hospital you were in my head,' he owned. 'Then I opened my eyes one day and there you were.' He paused, and suddenly the question she had once avoided was there again. 'Why did you come?' he asked.

'I—er...' She felt a great need to be honest with him. Silas appeared to be sharing the same piece of shaky ground, so whatever it might cost her, she felt an overwhelming urge to meet him halfway. 'The paper—the report in the paper said you were gravely ill.' She took a deep breath, held it for a moment, then, while her nerve held out, she plunged. 'And I'd begun to care for you too.'

'Sweetheart!' Silas breathed, and, his head coming closer, he gently kissed her. For ageless seconds they just stared at each other. Then Silas was saying, 'I have to confess that when I decided to leave hospital I did try to fight against the compulsion to ask you to come and stay at my place overnight.'

'Because...'

'Because I knew I was falling for you,' he admitted openly.

Did caring for her and falling for her mean that he loved her a little? She had no way, no experience, of knowing. The look in his eyes was warm, even tender, but... She started to feel a little scared. She decided to stick with that which she did know. 'But you did ask me to come. You phoned and—'

'And blamed my illness for my weakness. Had I been physically stronger I would not have been so otherwise weak.'

'You—um—gave in...?'

'I gave in,' he took up. 'And found I enjoyed having you tinkering about my apartment. That,' he added with a self-deprecating look, 'bothered me.'

'You were a bit of a snarly brute at times,' she said with a smile.

'Why wouldn't I be? I found I didn't want you to leave. Yet I wasn't ready to face what was happening to me.'

Colly looked solemnly at him. His caring for her, did he

mean? 'You sent me flowers,' she recalled, trying hard to keep her head together.

'I should have phoned to thank you,' he apologised. 'But I was a bit narked that you'd left without saying goodbye. I suppose to send you some "bread-and-butter" thank-you flowers was my bright idea of stamping "The End" on it.' He smiled then, a smile that made her heart turn over. 'Only it wasn't the end,' he said softly. 'The next time I saw you, you were having dinner with Andrews and appeared to be thoroughly enjoying his company.'

Colly stared at Silas in amazement. As he had picked up that note of jealousy in her voice, so she thought she detected something similar in his. 'You—were—jealous?' she asked in wonderment.

'There wasn't any shade of green that didn't bombard me,' he admitted. 'Oh, I fought against you, Colly Livingstone,' he went on, to thrill her some more. 'Even the next evening, when I was phoning you and asking you to have dinner with me, I fought against you.'

'Against your—caring for me?'

'Absolutely. Time and again I reminded myself that ours was a purely business arrangement, and that was the way it must be. And that while I might feel I should like to get to know you better, what would be the point? I did not want to be *married*-married.' He squeezed her hand and disclosed, 'I again made up my mind not to contact you again. I would resist all temptation to phone or see you again.' His eyes caressed her. 'Then you, my dear, dear, Colly, rang me,' he said, with such a tender look in his eyes for her that she had to swallow hard before she could find her voice.

'I rang to confess I'd done something terrible.'

'Poor love,' he breathed. 'And I knew that night, when I experienced feelings of such murderous rage when I imagined that Andrews had assaulted you, that I was in love with you.'

Her mouth fell open. His caring—was love! 'Oh, Silas!' she cried tremulously.

'It—doesn't—upset you that I feel so deeply for you?' he asked.

'Oh, no, not a bit,' she whispered. 'You're sure?' She could not believe it.

'I'm very sure,' he replied tenderly. 'I knew that night that I could fight it no longer. While I wasn't sure then what it was I did want—it was all new, too shattering—what I *was* sure about, without having to think about it, was that I would not mind the world knowing that you and I were married.'

'You wouldn't...?'

'I wouldn't.' He took a moment out to gently kiss her, but pulled back to ask, 'How do you feel about me, Colly?'

Looking at him, she felt nervous, and too shy to say those words she had never spoken before.

'You said that you care for me,' he said, when she did not answer, 'and I'm trying hard to go at a pace you're comfortable with. But I really would like to know something of the extent of you caring, little love.'

'I—er...' Colly gave a small cough to clear her choked throat. 'Oh, Silas Livingstone,' she managed, and, her voice strengthening, 'I've cried tonight because I thought my...the way I felt about you was hopeless. I...'

'Some of your tears were over me?'

'More than some, I think,' she acknowledged.

'My darling,' he breathed, and just had to tenderly kiss her, a loving hand stroking tenderly down the side of her face. 'Go on,' he urged gently, after some moments of just looking at her.

'I promise you I'm not someone who gives way to tears easily.' She obeyed, with what voice she could find. 'But as I drove away on our wedding day I could have burst into tears. I knew then that for all, as you'd remarked, we were not emotionally involved you were having a most peculiar effect on me.'

'Do you think it was the start of you—caring—for me?' Silas wanted to know.

'I tried to deny any such nonsense,' she replied with a

＊tender smile. 'But when I read in the paper about you being gravely ill, and I saw you in hospital, when, as exhausted as you were, you laughed at my "widow" comment—I knew then that I was very much in love with you.'

'Oh, Colly,' he groaned, and reached for her. And for seconds, wonderful long-short seconds, he held her in his arms. 'You're sure?' He leaned back to question her, as if he, like her, could not believe his hearing.

'I love you,' she answered huskily, a little self-consciously, and was drawn close up to him again.

For long blissful minutes they held each other, pulling back occasionally to tenderly kiss, then to break apart and, rejoicing, hold each other once more. 'I love you so very much, my beautiful wife,' Silas breathed against her ear.

'I love you so,' she replied. 'I never knew I could feel like this.'

'Sweetheart,' he said softly, and kissed her long and lingeringly before, breaking his kiss, he leaned away, his expression never more serious. 'Every hour since I parted from you yesterday has been pure torment.'

'Has it?' she asked softly, sympathetically. She had been there, and knew all about that torment.

'I never want to spend another torturous night like last night,' he said, smiling now at her, then going seriously on, 'I knew I would know no rest until I had seen you. That I would have to make contact with you this evening—then Naomi phoned and delayed me. When I saw you with Rupert—' Colly stiffened in his arms and he broke off. 'What?' he asked. 'Was it—?'

'Naomi?' Having revealed so much of her feelings, Colly saw no point in holding back now.

'What about her?' he asked, seeming mystified.

'Your date tonight…?'

'*Date!* She wasn't my…! Oh, Lord, didn't I say?' He did a fast backtrack over his remarks with regard to Naomi. Then, with a groan, 'I didn't!' he exclaimed. 'Oh, my love, I've been so stewed up over you. So scared of frightening you away should I get to talk of love with you, that I completely forgot. I'm so sorry,' he apologised, but went quickly on to enlighten her, 'Naomi is Kit's wife.'

'Kit? Your cousin Kit?'

'One and the same. But let me explain. I had a meeting in Lisbon today—I was scheduled to stay over and return in the morning, but I was anxious to see you.' Already Colly was feeling dreadful about her jealousy. Poor darling, he must be tired out. He had declined to stay in Portugal because he had wanted to see her!

'You don't have to explain,' she told him hurriedly.

But he was not having that. 'I think I do,' he contradicted softly. 'I don't want any misunderstandings between us,' he said, going on, 'I'd barely got home, and was wondering whether to phone first or just call on you, when Naomi rang sounding extremely upset and asking if I would meet her to discuss a problem. It seemed churlish to say no. Kit being family makes Naomi family. I said I'd meet her for a coffee somewhere—anything more would take too long. She suggested an establishment that was close to her. "Our" hotel. I would have preferred somewhere else, but she seemed under enough pressure without me giving her further problems.'

'Were you able to help her?'

Silas shook his head. 'I doubt it. She may feel better for having sounded off about Kit's misdemeanours—she's fairly certain he's having an affair—but, while I'll have a word with him, I doubt anything I can say will make the smallest difference. But that's enough about a marriage that's going wrong. I'd prefer to talk about a marriage that I dearly hope will from now on start to go right.'

Oh, heavens! Colly wished she knew more of what he meant. She gave herself a mental shake. For goodness' sake, this was a man who, after what she knew would have been a full day of business, had dashed back to London because he was anxious to see *her*!

'*Our*—marriage?' she asked tentatively.

'Don't be scared, love,' Silas said gently. 'I mean our marriage. If you need more time, I'll wait. If you still want a career, that's fine. But I have to tell you that I love you so much it is my dearest wish that we make our marriage a permanent and a proper marriage.'

She looked at him, her heart thundering away. 'By p-permanent and proper, you mean…' Her voice faded.

Silas looked back at her steadily. 'By permanent and proper I mean I want you to come and live with me and be my wife,' he answered quietly. And when, with roaring in her ears, Colly stared at him speechlessly, 'I want you to be my wife—' He broke off, then, his eyes holding hers, added, 'In every sense of the word, Colly.'

She had an idea she had gone a touch pink, but his eyes were still quietly holding hers. 'But—but you don't want to do anything that in the long term will bind us together. You said so. On Saturday.' She clearly remembered. 'When we first went to our room, you said—'

'I lied,' he cut in.

'You—lied?' she queried, and just had to burst out laughing.

But Silas did not laugh. 'You're all right about that side of marriage?' he asked carefully. 'I won't rush you. If you…'

A light all at once started to dawn. 'Without wishing to sound too forward, I believe I'm very all right with—um—that side,' she murmured, wondering, after her response to him yesterday, how he could doubt it. 'I love you,' she told him solemnly. And, when he held her that little bit closer, yet still seemed a tiny bit unsure, 'I love you so much, Silas. I want you with my heart, with my mind, and with my body.'

He stared at her for ageless moments, then drew her yet closer up to him. He kissed her then, and it was a wonderful kiss, a kiss that was vastly different from the gentle tender kisses they had shared that evening.

Her heart was racing furiously when with gently seeking fingers his hand found its way inside the light wrap she wore, and as gently he cupped her breast in his hand.

'Oh, Silas!' she whispered, on a small gulp of breath.

He stilled. 'Oh, Silas, yes? Or, Oh, Silas, no?' he asked gently.

She looked at him, puzzled. But as he wanted no misunderstandings between them, neither did she. 'Yes,' she murmured shyly.

'Darling,' he said softly, and a little raggedly. 'I feel as if I'm treading on eggshells here—you said no yesterday...'

'No, I didn't,' she denied. Silas pulled back from her, taking his hand away from her breast and drawing the edges of her wrap together. 'When did I?' she asked. Her memory of it was...

'When I—'

'Oh!' she exclaimed, as all at once she recalled his fingers on the material of her nightdress.

'Oh?'

She went a little pink again. 'You'll have to forgive me,' she said quietly. 'I'm new to all of this.' But, determined as he, her dear love, to have no misunderstandings, she overcame her feeling of shyness to own, 'I wasn't saying no, I didn't want to—er—make love with you.' His words 'I don't want to worry or upset you' and 'I'm doing my best to be restrained, here' took on a new meaning, 'Oh, Silas. You said something about me not needing my nightie. I've never been naked in front of a man before. I couldn't hack it.' She coughed self-consciously. 'I seem to have a bit of a hangup... I just couldn't... B-but otherwise... That's what I meant! Not...' She felt very warm all at once.

'Oh, my sweet love,' Silas burst in. 'What an insensitive clod I am!' he grieved. 'Forgive me. I should have realised...'

'It doesn't matter. Not now,' she assured him. How could anything matter any more? Silas loved her and she loved him. Silas loved her, loved *her*.

'We won't make it matter,' he decreed. 'It's a minor obstacle that will pass as we get to know each other.' He smiled then, a wonderful smile. And then asked, 'Are you going to marry me, Mrs Livingstone? Are you going to live with me, and love with me, and stay—permanently—married to me?'

She smiled a beautiful smile; she had never been so happy. 'I'm so glad you came back from Lisbon,' she replied, love shining from her eyes. 'The answer, Mr Livingstone, is yes.'

Their smiles became grins, tender loving grins. 'Wife,' he said softly, as if savouring the sound. 'My wife,' he said lovingly. 'My extra-special—wife.'

If you enjoyed what you just read,
then we've got an offer you can't resist!

Take 2 bestselling
love stories FREE!
Plus get a FREE surprise gift!

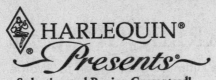

HARLEQUIN®
Presents

Seduction and Passion Guaranteed!

Legally wed, but he's never said…
"I love you."

They're…

Wedlocked!

The series
in which
marriages are
made in haste…
and love
comes later…

**Look out for more Wedlocked! marriage stories
in Harlequin Presents throughout 2005.**

Coming in May:
THE DISOBEDIENT BRIDE
by Helen Bianchin
#2463

Coming in June:
THE MORETTI MARRIAGE
by Catherine Spencer
#2474